D1527743

About My Murder

A soft-boiled detective story

Stan Burroway

Book design by Debby Schoeningh/The Country Side Press
Cover design by Jenna Hubert
Editor: Debby Schoeningh
Published in Reno, Nevada and printed in the U.S.A.

ISBN: 9798598519455
Library of Congress Control Number: 2021901420

For Janet
—at last

DISCLAIMER, OF SORTS

This story is a work of fiction, but it is set in five specific days of early May 1968 and refers to real places as they were then, and, in passing, to real public figures and events in that contentious year of social change. Nevertheless, all of the private characters in the story are fictional and any resemblance to any actual persons living or dead is purely coincidental. And If that were not true the author would still insist on it because in California there is no statute of limitations on murder. Years of reading teach us that most biographies contain more fiction than their authors are even aware of, and most works of fiction are more autobiographical than their authors will ever admit.

1.

I picked up the girl in Los Gatos, and that made all the difference.

When I came out of the gas station she was standing in the sunshine near the highway, dressed, like someone's idea of a farmer's daughter, in rolled-up jeans and a blue work shirt. It was hard to miss the way she filled the jeans or the way she had tied up the shirttails in front, leaving a bare midriff and what seemed like enough room to write "Available" in 60-point type. She was in her mid-twenties probably–we still called them "girls" in those days–a brunette, with the Jackie Kennedy bouffant hair some of them were still wearing.

She was petite and pretty, yes, but oddly just right and all wrong, too pale for the California sunshine, too delicate for her work clothes, too much eye makeup for morning along this rural road. It was pretty clear that she needed to be taken to some other place.

As for me, I was the Man of Mystery that day–definitely not myself–driving a borrowed Porsche to a borrowed beach house on Monterey Bay for what, up until then, had been planned as a weekend of solitude.

So of course I knew exactly the difference she would make.

Well, I was wrong about that.

* * *

I had left San Francisco at about nine-thirty, that Saturday morning, driving west through Golden Gate Park, then south through the stucco in the Sunset District, past

1

the concrete apartment towers of Park Merced, and out to the hills of Daly City with their ticky-tacky houses, the little boxes in the Joan Baez song. My plan was to take Skyline Boulevard along the spine of the Peninsula to miss the towns and traffic on Bayshore and my own heavy demons on Highway One along the Pacific.

The Porsche was a year-old silver gray 911 coupe. Skyline was made for it, the day was made to give it a run, and after the first fifteen minutes or so I was made to be its driver.

This side of Switzerland, there weren't many two-lane roads more beautiful than Skyline Boulevard on that green morning in 1968. It snaked through the hills far above the red tile roofs of Stanford, a set of seductive curves matching the convex-concave shapes of the land itself. Seagulls hung and slid on the ocean breeze, evergreen forests, reservoirs and fruit orchards flashed past in the sunshine, white fences unreeled, and at the wing window the wind whispered, *rich rich rich*! The air smelled of sea salt, pine trees and fruit blossoms, and the land seemed to roll as if all the wealth in the state was bubbling up underneath and wouldn't lie flat for anyone.

But the trip to Monterey is more than 120 miles, so when Skyline ended and the plum trees parted just enough for a dozen or so sleepy blocks of Los Gatos, I slowed down and pulled into a service station for some Chevron Supreme and the spotless restroom.

It was when I came out that I first saw her; she was looking my way and resting one white tennis shoe on a long green metal case, a sort of toolbox. She gave me a slow smile. I smiled back and paid the kid in the white cap. Then, since I had to drive right by her to get back to the highway, I braked, leaned across the passenger seat and said, "Hi."

"Hi!" She bent to look through the window. "If you're driving south, I'd sure like to ride along."

"If you'd like to ride along, I'd drive south even if I was heading north."

She pointed her index finger up, then leveled it at me. "Cute!" she said with a grin, tipped the seat forward to slide the green box behind it, and got in.

I couldn't believe my luck.

When she settled into the bucket seat beside me, I got a faint whiff of light perfume–the best scent of the day so far just because there was a woman in it.

"My name's Misty," she said.

Perfect.

"I'm Dan," I told her, even though I wasn't. If she wasn't going to give me her full name, I wasn't going to give her my real one. And you might as well know, reader, that I don't intend to give it to you either, for reasons you may understand later.

Telling the truth was my nature and my occupation, too–I'm a newspaperman–so keeping my name from a pretty girl on a pretty morning was something that would have been on my conscience ordinarily. But, that day, driving that sporty car, I was someone else, the Man of Mystery: the Man with the Porsche.

Having the Porsche for the weekend was really a last-minute fluke. My pal, Scott Croswell, and I had been meeting for breakfast almost every Tuesday since January, just after my wife, Laura, had died in an awful single car crash on the Coast Highway. Scott was our dentist, that's how we met him, but he'd become a good friend to both of us, probably my best friend outside of work. He was shaken by Laura's death and I think he wanted to keep track of how I was doing. It was like him to care enough to stay around after some of our other friends had sent sympathy cards and forgotten my phone number.

Just out of dental school, Scott had joined a practice down the coast in Monterey. Several years ago he had left that office to open his own in San Francisco, but he'd hung onto his Monterey beach house to use on weekends. Early in April, he offered it to me, just to get away by myself for a few days and focus on putting my life back together. He had this book, "Living with a Loss," that he said I really should read. "It was given to me after my dad died years ago. I'll lend it to you. Go down there and put your feet up and take it easy for a couple of days," he told me. "It's pretty clear you need a break, pal."

Eventually I said yes. When Laura was still alive, we'd planned way ahead to take a vacation week in early May to drive up the coast to Oregon, and that week off was still scheduled at work, but I'd scrubbed the Oregon trip, and going south would be better now, even if just for a long weekend.

My first day away was going to be Saturday, May 4th. On Thursday Scott called me in the early afternoon, just before I left for my shift at the *Record*: "Hey, Killer, (he called all his pals that) I just had a great idea! On Saturday I've got to move old file boxes out of the office and into a storage unit, seven of 'em. It's one of the things keeping me in the city this weekend. There's no way they'll fit in my car. I was thinking I'd have to rent a van, but you've got that station wagon. Why don't you take my Porsche down to Monterey and lend me your Ford? We'll trade back Monday afternoon–it's an offer you can't refuse!"

He was right–I couldn't. When you came across a Porsche in the Bay Area back in 1968, you couldn't help noticing. There weren't that many around. In San Francisco then a big black Cadillac sedan suggested that the owner was wealthy, old and conservative, but a little silver Porsche, which cost just as much, said that the driver was probably rich, young and adventurous. That was my message for this weekend, anyway, and now with a pretty girl tucked in beside me, I was going to be all of those.

2.

Misty swiveled toward me in her seat as if for an intimate chat. She had the advantage. Most of the time, I had to have eyes on the road.

"How far are you planning to go? I asked.

"As far as you want." (My heart jumped at that.) "I'm just trying to get to L.A."

"Well, I'm only driving down to Monterey for a weekend at a beach house. It's not direct to L.A., but it's a start south. Why L.A.? What do you do?"

"I'm a professional dancer."

"Really? Movies and TV?"

"No, what makes you ask that?"

"Well, L.A. is where it all is, and you're certainly pretty enough."

"Thank you."

"I'd bet TV is where you'll end up, unless you're in a ballet troupe or modern dance or something. I hope TV isn't an insult."

"No, I dance in the club scene mostly."

"But you're traveling light?

Her answer was unexpectedly bitter.

"*Now* I am! I left San Francisco with a suitcase and a big purse, but my jerk-ass ex-boyfriend robbed me last night."

"Robbed you?"

"When we stopped at a motel on the edge of Los Gatos. He was going to drive me all the way to L.A. along the coast–anyway that's what he said. But you can't trust men–they're all the same, all assholes. Sorry, Dan, I don't mean you–I don't know you. But anyway, when I woke up, he was gone with everything I had–suitcase, purse, even my cigarettes–and the purse had at least six hundred bucks, not to mention all my ID. How lame is that? The first thing I'll have to do in L.A. is find the damn DMV for a new license." She tossed her hands open in exasperation. "Oh shit, and Social Security too! I'll need it to get hired. He left me nothing but my bait box; there was nothing to do but pick it up and look for a ride south.

"Bait box? So do you like to fish?"

"God, no–well, sort of." she gave me a sly look. "The bait box is for my cosmetics. 'Holds things a dancer needs–plus a few dollars my dork-face ex-boy-friend, Leroy, didn't know about, thank God!"

"You didn't try to go after him?"

"Leroy? Not a chance–he's bad news. Dangerous! Besides, he's probably given my clothes away to a new girl already."

I didn't like hearing that, but I shrugged off the uneasy feeling it gave me.

Her language surprised me, too. I had been in the Army and I worked in a newsroom, so I'd heard worse, but not often from a woman–not in those days. And another thing struck me as odd, so I asked, "You were only taking one suitcase? Doesn't a girl like you need more clothes than that?"

"Sure, except at work. I sent two suitcases and a big box of stuff ahead by Greyhound Express, to pick up in Will Call at the L.A. bus terminal. I don't have an address down there yet. As for dancing, the shoes take up more room than the bikinis, that's for sure."

I decided to match her breezy attitude. "Then you're a go-go girl?"

"Um hmm!" She tilted her chin up proudly.

"You dance topless?"

"Uh huh, topless, bottomless–depends on the club and the county and who's watching–Hey, are you *blushing*?" She giggled and I tried to cover.

"Maybe, but don't think anything of it. I blush at card tricks."

I didn't dwell on my embarrassment long, because I was thinking that Misty had obviously run with some fairly rough characters already. For all I knew she had a nice little pistol in that bait box behind her bucket seat and was planning to rob me and take off in Scott's car. Maybe Leroy was even in on it.

But I stole another look at her and saw how ridiculous that was. She was a kid making her way in the world on good looks and moxie. Fate, I decided, had handed me a damsel in distress. Out of town now, I was watching the road and shifting down as we began to climb, heading south toward Santa Cruz, but I caught her looking me over too, apparently deciding I was okay.

I was a six-footer then, 31 years old, my hobby was running, and except for ears that stick out a little too much, my features were all in the right place, so I probably looked at least as good as the businessmen and tourists who hunkered down next to the stage when she danced.

"Do you have a deadline to get to L.A.?" I asked.

"No, just to look for a club and a job. No one's expecting me, but I'll get hired easy enough. The hard part will be getting the Social Security and driver's license again."

So–why not? I was used to making quick changes in plans. "Then, if you'd like to, you could stay at the beach house with me until I head back to the city Monday. It's a nice place. I could take you into Salinas on Highway 101–that's about 20 miles inland. There's a Greyhound station there, and Southern Pacific too, and they both go to L.A. I could lend you the fare."

"Oh… Um… Okay! But I need to get a dress and shoes somewhere. I put this on for the drive yesterday and it's all I've got today."

"Well, we'll be in Santa Cruz in about half an hour and I guess I could spring for that–there's a Penney's there, anyway–will that do?"

"Sure, I grew up in Penney's."

"You know what? If you go Greyhound, you'll end up right where you sent your clothes."

She considered that and frowned a little.

"Yes, but I don't have a place to take my stuff yet, and a train ride would be fun. I've never been on a train. I've had enough Greyhound the last few years–all the way from Nebraska to Sacramento."

"Why did you start in Nebraska?"

"Why does anybody? I was born there."

"So, why did you leave?"

She scowled and shifted toward her window, then back toward me. "To ditch my so-called family and so-called school. My dad had a farm just outside a town on the highway west of Grand Island. My mom died when I was four and my brother was seven."

"I'm sorry."

"Yeah. By the time I was eight, we were doing farm jobs till sundown except for school time. For a while my brother sort of took care of me, but when I got to be 15–he was 18–he got to be a real pain. He thought he owned me and didn't treat me fair, not even close."

I thought I knew what she was getting at.

"Couldn't you complain to someone?" I stole another glance and saw a look of distaste.

"To my dad. He popped my brother around pretty good,

so from then on Bud really hated me. That was okay with me–for a while–but my dad wasn't really on my side all that much. And the town girls at school–the cheerleaders, who weren't even that pretty–started being really mean."

"Why was that?" She didn't answer for a second, staring out the window at empty land going past.

"Oh, mainly because I was dating the fullback on the team. He was a town boy–grocer's son–so they thought he belonged to them. Just jealous! Those fat pigs whispered around some nasty lies about me and about my brother and dad both! That's when I decided to take off–my senior year was half over already anyway."

"That was pretty brave."

"Yeah, I was broke but I got lunch money for school, so I made myself sack lunches every day when Dad and Bud were out working in a field. I hid 'em near the stop for the school bus. Then instead of eating cafeteria, I saved until I had twelve bucks. I wore extra clothes to school and stuffed 'em in my locker 'till I had a whole black plastic bag full. Then one morning I went to school on the bus, got the bag out of my locker and walked a couple of blocks to the Greyhound stop. I caught the bus going east to the Greyhound station in Grand Island and bought a ticket going west to Denver there. Then I rode right back past my school and our farm and kept going to Colorado."

"But weren't you still just about broke?"

"Well, I'd turned 18, and a lady in a Denver coffee shop hired me to wash dishes. Dishwashing didn't last long. Her husband was the owner. He told his wife, 'She's *way* too pretty to be working in the back!' So I started waitressing–getting tips. About a year later I got a better waitress job at a roadhouse. And it wasn't long after that till topless dancing came to Denver. *That* was an education."

"I bet, " I said.

"I mean about the money. I like dancing. I'm a natural–all the guys say that. My tips the first night were as much as a week at the coffee shop! After that I just kept going west for better jobs–a casino in Elko, then a club in Sacramento, then San Francisco. But I didn't have to take the bus to San Francisco. A very nice gentleman drove me."

"And now you're going to L.A.?"

She leaned forward excitedly as if she wanted to arrive that much sooner. "Word gets around. Clubs are opening all the time by the military factories and aerospace plants. They're building space capsules there! Extra hours and big pay! I hear the tips are great."

"You know," I said, "I was in on the very start of the topless craze when San Francisco kicked it off three or four years ago. It was just about the third night after it began at the Condor Club. Their star had this act where she came down from the ceiling dancing on a grand piano. They lowered it on cables.

"She'd been doing it every night in a bikini, but this time she wore one of those black topless bathing suits that were new from Europe that summer, the ones with just those real narrow straps that crossed in front."

"How'd you happen to be there, huh?"

"My wife read about it in Herb Caen's column in the *Chronicle* and said, 'Let's go see for ourselves!' Broadway was so close we could walk there from our apartment, so we did–the very first week. In a month topless go-go dancing and topless barmaids were all over town, and other cities were catching on."

Misty's tone was frosty, "So…. you're married?"

"Was. My wife died in a road accident about three months ago."

"Oh, I'm so sorry! God, Dan, I'm sorry." I caught her

sincere, sorrowful look; it ended with her lips puckered as if for a kiss.

"Thank you. Yeah–not that far from here, really. Laura went off Highway One over on the coast near Devil's Slide–night and foggy and she always was sort of a pedal-to-the-metal driver. The fog rolls in there and you can be in the clear one minute and, like, lost in a cloud the next."

Sunny day or not, gloom always descended on me whenever I had to tell the story to someone who didn't yet know. Laura had been trying to get a foothold as a serious modern artist. She was on her way back to San Francisco from a gallery opening in Carmel that night, alone because I had a late shift at work. I was home by midnight and had already gone to sleep when the Highway Patrol called.

"I got out there about daybreak," I said. "'Slow going in the fog on the coast."

"Oh God! Poor you."

"Laura drove an old VW bug–white one. 'Looked like a broken eggshell down there in the rocks and the surf–both doors open, hood smashed. The tides and waves are pretty strong there–divers tried but they couldn't find her in that churning ocean."

Misty's forehead wrinkled and her eyes were wide. "That must have been *terrible* for you!"

"Yeah. 'Felt pretty smashed up myself that morning. One CHP guy drove me all the way back to my apartment in San Francisco in the patrol car, and his partner followed driving mine."

I had called the San Mateo County Sheriff later that day and they told me divers would be working there at low tides the next two days, so I went down both days to watch–one dive director on the sand and two guys in a boat, along with two divers in wet suits and snorkel stuff, but it was no use–they finally gave up.

"That's why I took Skyline today," I told Misty. "There's a guard rail where it happened now, but I don't take the Coast Road anymore. And the Bayshore Freeway is usually a mess."

"Still, you're doing okay?"

"Well, a lot better. We had a little memorial service for her, about two dozen people: some of our friends, folks from my work, artists she knew. They told me I did Laura proud."

"You have anyone to talk to?"

"Yeah, our friend Scott–he's was our dentist–and then Jerry Grimes, my best friend at work. Jerry's older and single, but he had younger brother about my age who died in a hunting accident last year in Wyoming. 'Bad one–shotgun. About two weeks after Laura's funeral, I helped Jerry move his stuff from one apartment to another and we talked a lot that day. He told me that being in one of those grief-support groups had helped him keep going. So I tried it–just an hour and a half once a week–and it turned out I liked it. You know, at first the others help you get through whatever you're feeling. Later you realize you're trying to help the newer people yourself, and that's when you figure you're starting to get better."

"Yeah? Gee."

I didn't see any reason to tell her more, not about how I had struggled with guilt at first, because, after seven years, the marriage was not what I had expected. And, because our daily schedules were so different and we had so little time together, I sometimes imagined myself in relationships with someone new.

I had met Laura at a freshman mixer the first week of college and fell for her from the first. She was a blonde beauty, cherub-faced and innocent looking, but not dumb by any means; her sharp blue eyes and a quick wit suggested that innocence wasn't the whole story. After I first spotted her, I hung back for ten minutes trying to work up courage, but then I thought "what the hell" and I was about as forward as I had ever been. I just walked up and said, "Well, hello, stranger!"

She cocked her head: "Do I know you?"

"Not at all. That's why I called you stranger. But I'd *like* to know you."

She gave me a faint smile. "Is this how you always meet girls?"

"I never meet girls. But it's a mixer, so I'm mixing–trying anyway."

"Well, you get points for trying. What's your name?"

And just like that, we were friends, and then close friends all through college, and eventually a married couple, with all the complications that brought.

Ten years later, my wife had been as attractive as ever. I'd been proud to go into a restaurant with her; I thought we probably made a 'good-looking couple.' But her look had changed some, more guarded I thought. By then she was having to compete for gallery space and trying to sell her own paintings without an agent, so maybe that was part of it.

And by then we were on different tracks. Though much of her art wasn't to my taste, Laura had some talent and truly hoped to be recognized. I wanted us to have children–old story. I thought we could have both–yes, artists need time to work, but they don't have to keep office hours, and if anyone would be willing to take care of kids, I would. Dads who really pitched in to help seemed to be the new thing. Girls or boys, I'd do my share and more. My job at the paper didn't even start till 3:30 in the afternoon most days, so she'd have all day until then to paint. All my schedule meant at the moment was that we didn't have a whole lot of romantic evenings together. So after the accident I blamed myself for not having loved her enough, or maybe often enough, in what turned out to be the last months we had.

"So the group therapy stuff really helps?" Misty asked.

"Yes, a lot. That kind of surprised me. Keeping really busy at your job helps too."

"What job is that? It must pretty classy if you have a beach house and a Porsche."

"Not really. I'm a copyeditor–I work for the *San Francisco Record Courier.* I check news stories to make sure they're right and ready to print, write headlines for them–all that sort of stuff."

"Ohhh." Her disappointment was obvious., but then her face brightened. "Can you get to be a reporter?"

I hid my irritation. "It works the other way around, usually. I *was* a reporter a couple of years ago, but I'm hoping eventually to be an assignment editor–those editors decide which stories to cover, and they're partners with reporters, but sort of in charge."

"Um hum. But if you have a Porsche…"

I finally decided to come clean; lying for long always made me uncomfortable anyway.

"Not mine. I'm borrowing the car and the beach house both from my pal, Scott Croswell, the dentist we hung out with. I've got some time off and Scott needed a car over the weekend with enough space to move cartons of stuff. So we traded, the Porsche for my Ford Station Wagon. He gets this car back Monday afternoon."

Misty said, "Um…" I figured I'd just done my best to talk myself out of an easy romance.

3.

It was warm for early May. We drove across the 20 miles of high plateau between Los Gatos and Santa Cruz–not as scenic as Skyline, but to the west we could see distant hills covered with evergreens. Near the road there was open land and fields with banked rows ready to be planted in strawberries. In a yard in front of one large house two men in blue jeans were painting a newly built fruit stand. One of them, on a ladder, was lettering a big white sign in red. So far it spelled BER...

For someone who'd been robbed just hours before, Misty didn't seem to be much put out; it looked like she was enjoying the drive without a care. "I haven't been out of the city for months," she said, "and I never was in a Porsche before." The road ahead was straight and empty, so I stepped harder on the gas for a minute. The engine growled aggressively, we shot forward, and Misty whooped with delight.

The forest grew closer for a while and, after a curve, we suddenly could look down on Monterey Bay, like a big bite out of the California Coast, with sunny Santa Cruz below us on the north side and the old city of Monterey, just out of sight today, 20 or more miles away–on the south coast, facing north.

"That's really gorgeous!" Misty said, shading her eyes from the sun.

"After we go to Penney's we'll get some lunch," I said. "Then we'll buy groceries. Scott says there's almost nothing in his fridge. He stocks up in Santa Cruz on the way down."

I began to figure out what two of us would need for dinner tonight, three meals tomorrow and breakfast again Monday, and to make a plan. Five beach house meals across the table from her, and two nights in the only bed, would more than make up for the dent to my wallet.

Penney's turned out to be a bit more of a shopping expedition than I counted on. Misty left with a pair of black high-heeled shoes, some bikini panties, about $30 worth of bras (size 36C, she told me) and two spring frocks–she couldn't decide between the sharp red and white pinstripe and the white, purple, and yellow floral print. She had come out of the dressing room to model each of them for me and, yes, they were both fetching. "They're both on sale," she told me. "Can't we just get them both?" Well, of course we could.

After that, and an hour later than I'd expected, we had iced tea and sand dabs at a fish shack restaurant right on the beach. The table was tiny, which was fine with me; as we talked, I could stare up close at her bright brown eyes, fake lashes and the dark mascara that went with her big bouffant hair. She ate daintily, but as if she hadn't had a meal in two days. And she kept me chatting while she put away everything on her plate.

"So what's the deal with your Porsche friend?" she asked me.

"Scott's a prince, he's been really great to me since Laura died. His dental office is doing pretty well, and I guess you'd call him a man about town. He goes to some of the big charity dances, gives donations, all that. Anyway, just out of dental school he started with an office in Monterey, but then he moved to San Francisco and picked up a lot of high society type clients. Now he has a nice business in a classy old building on Green Street.'

"So he gives away money?"

"Well, he seems to be making it fast enough, but he's from a family in New York–they lived in the Hudson Valley, not the city–and I take it that his father was pretty well off, so there was money to start with, and that doesn't hurt."

It was Laura who had seen Scott Croswell pictured in the *Record's* society pages and had decided to try him for a filling she needed. She liked his office and staff, and when he charged her no more than other dentists, she talked me into seeing him too. It turned out that he was interested in both modern art and the local newspapers, so we had things to talk about. Before long he invited us out for a fish dinner at the noisy Tadish Grill.

"That was so much fun!" Laura said on the cable car home. "We need to pay him back with dinner right away."

I told her that would be pricey, but she said, "I'll cook." And, to my delight, she did–the best pork roast and rice she'd ever served. I thought our little apartment was nothing special for someone who made the society pages, but Scott seemed right at home. After dinner he sat on our couch, threw his arms up on the back and, without giving any names, told tales about the foibles of his wealthier patients, like the skittish matron who insisted she'd only have a cavity filled if she could bring her Pekinese into the office and hold him on her lap to keep her calm. Not a good idea. The drill excited the dog, the dog wet on the woman and the woman left red-faced and in tears. She never came back, so Scott lost a client, but he laughed about it.

One Sunday six weeks after our dinner, Scott invited us to a cocktail party at his swell bachelor's pad in Monterey. Two of his guests turned out to be gallery owners from

Carmel, and that had been a break for Laura. Both of those galleries had put a painting or two of hers on display and she got a couple of small sales.

"We were lucky to get to know him," I said.

"And you still hang out with him now?" Misty asked.

"Yeah, I do, Tuesday breakfasts, mostly. After Laura's accident, I went down for two days to watch the divers search for her body. The second day was a Saturday and Scott didn't have office hours, so he offered to go along. He even drove–that was the first time I was ever in this car. It was good to have him with me because it was a downer when the divers couldn't find her and gave up. He suggested the Tuesday breakfasts on the ride back. Just two or three weeks after that, I needed four wisdom teeth pulled and when I got Scott's bill it was about half of what it should have been. I protested, but he said to forget it."

I heard myself and thought maybe I sounded cheap, but Misty nodded. "Nice guy."

I paid for lunch and we headed to Safeway. We came out of there with a cartful: steaks, baking potatoes, hamburger, salad stuff, bacon, eggs, four red apples. milk, frozen orange juice, bread, jelly, sliced ham, a small bottle of mayo, a quart of chocolate ice cream, four bottles of red wine, and three packs of cigarettes for Misty. I'd spent lots more than I'd planned on this trip so far, and the banks would be closed now until Monday morning. In those days, before most folks had credit cards, and ATMs hadn't yet come to the West Coast, out-of-town cash was hard to come by on weekends. But I still had about fifty bucks, probably twice as much as I'd need for Misty's train fare to L.A.

When we rolled the basket out to the parking lot beside the store, three kids, aged maybe 12 to 14, were giving the Porsche a close inspection, but keeping hands off.

"Hi, guys," I said. "Like it?"

"Yeah!" two of them said, grinning.

"Well, study hard and maybe you'll buy one yourself someday."

The older boys looked skeptical, the youngest wide-eyed and hopeful, but Misty grinned, and I winked at her. She was standing by the car, already lighting a cigarette, as I stowed the last of the food, and I couldn't help noticing how the oldest boy's attention had already shifted from the Porsche to Misty. She noticed too and brushed her hair back with clasped hands behind her head as she leaned back a bit to blow her first puff of smoke at the sky, a pose that didn't detract at all from her figure.

As any boy in his teens could see, I was one lucky millionaire that day.

4.

Out of Santa Cruz we followed Highway One along the coast for probably 40 miles in a big sweep to the southeast, then southwest, with the Pacific always on Misty's side of the car. At Moss Landing, the fresh smell of the sea and the tall twin stacks of the PG&E power plant told me that we were on the last leg of the trip.

As we came closer to Scott's beach house, my plans for the evening ahead became more real to me, and, to be honest, that made me uneasy. Despite her simplicity, I thought, Misty was entirely comfortable being a perfect sex symbol–a pro at that job. That made me an amateur–celibate for more than three months now and, even though I had my fantasies, loyal to one woman all my life. An Army top sergeant told me once that my strong conscience was my worst weakness, and I guess that was true now. When I thought about what was ahead, my mouth went dry and I could have used a sip of the wine we'd just bought.

But while I secretly stewed a bit, Misty was just taking in the scenery. "What are they growing there?" she asked as we passed fields of large plants with spiky green leaves. "I never saw a crop like that before."

"Artichokes. They like the sea air. They're a really big deal in this part of California." Almost immediately we came to a bypass at the edge of a town, and a sign announcing "Castroville, Artichoke Capital of the World." "See?" I said, "We take them seriously."

We took the long drive past, or really through, Fort

Ord, acres and acres of identical wooden barracks behind cyclone fences, with squads of men, Saturday work details probably, in olive-drab fatigues marching on my side of the car and a string of empty rifle ranges facing sand dunes and the sea on Misty's.

"After I was drafted, I had basic training here." I said. "Sixteen really long weeks in 1961, then they sent me to Germany."

"You went to Germany?

"Yeah, that was a roll of the dice; 'could've been sent anywhere, even to Vietnam; we were about to have our first troops there, back when the Army pretended they were just advisers. But I got lucky, and I was in Deutschland for 16 months–drafted, just out of college, just married. Just a few months later, Laura followed me over and we rented rooms from a German family near my base. After that, army duty turned out to be pretty good for us. We used my leave time to go to Rome and London."

"No kidding? Everyone I know said the army was the pits."

South of the fort, in Seaside, we drove a couple of miles through stoplights on busy Del Monte Boulevard, until a sign marked the Monterey city limits. A small hill that appeared to be part sand dune began to rise on our right and at the second stop sign I made a right turn, across a single set of railroad spur tracks. Immediately the road became steep and climbed to the hilltop, where I turned right again on a street called Dunecrest, then swung left around an acre or two of eucalyptus trees that separated Scott's house from all the others clustered on the dunes nearer downtown. A sign on one tree announced: "Private Drive" and in fact the road ended abruptly.

The beach house wasn't impressive at first glance–a long, low box with a flat roof that we approached from the back across a wide apron of blacktop, so all we could see was a wide overhead door to a two-car garage and a redwood wall to the right, broken only by clearstory windows and a back door. But I knew better than to go in by that door. Instead, I put the overhead door up and drove into the big empty garage. Misty frowned, pouted really, as she swung her legs out of the car and followed me into the house by a door that led to a small and plain laundry room with an automatic washer and dryer. I was enjoying her disappointment because I didn't think it would last. Then we went into the kitchen.

The kitchen was just one corner of a huge room, nearly twice the size of the garage. An L-shaped island with a white tile top separated it from a steel and mahogany dining table and the rest of the expensively furnished space. Across the floor of big, dark red Mission tile, the real front of the entire house was a 30-foot stretch of floor-to-ceiling glass, facing a redwood deck and a panoramic view of the bay.

Misty had an open-mouth smile. "This is so cool!"

A black leather couch, in front of a used-brick wall at the far end of the room, faced a Persian rug, a heavy glass-topped coffee table and a matching black leather armchair.

I gave Misty a quick tour. On the back wall, next to the kitchen and a wet bar, were three doors, first to a big walk-in closet, then to the bath–windowless, but with a large skylight–and last to the only bedroom, with the door to the outside that we had seen driving in.

Back at the big window in the front room, I unlatched the sliding glass door, and Misty and I went out to stand on the deck, smell the sea and look at the bay, dark blue in the afternoon light. The empty beach, sand right up to the house, fell away quickly beneath the deck and then sloped gently into the water.

In her jeans and blue shirt, Misty leaned on the railing, staring.

"What do you think?" I asked.

She lit a cigarette. "It beats Nebraska."

We brought the groceries in and stored them in the steel cabinets and the harvest gold refrigerator. As Scott had promised, the fridge was almost empty except for soda cans and some half-full bottles of salad dressing. When Misty got her new clothes out of the Porsche and carried them to the bedroom closet, I dropped my gym bag beside the queen-sized bed, feeling satisfied with my prospects but a little uneasy; Scott's book on loss was inside and I knew it was unlikely to be read this weekend.

Back in the kitchen we opened one of the bottles of pinot noir we'd bought and settled down to talk across the dining room table.

Misty looked at me intently. "Your friend has a swell house. I can't believe he would just give it to you for the weekend–and his car too."

"Scott's always been generous. 'Matter of fact, his only condition was that I shouldn't tell anyone that he was lending me the place. He didn't want that to get back to some of his friends who hinted they'd like to borrow it. 'Said they drank a lot and he didn't really trust them not to trash it."

"So you're special?"

"More special since Laura died, maybe."

It was true. Scott Croswell had thought of Laura as a close friend. On the Saturday when the divers tried again at low tide and Scott drove us down, we got to the narrow beach in late morning and stayed till the tide swamped the rocks and the divers gave up for good about four in the afternoon. I hadn't asked Scott to go with me, but with his office closed for the weekend, he offered. So we were closer after that. Because I had few evenings free it was his idea to meet for Tuesday breakfasts.

"He's an upbeat guy," I told Misty, "and he tells me I need to move on. He suggested the beach house weekend so I could just drop out a bit."

"Drop out?"

"Well, get my breath. There's Laura, and then you can probably guess what this year has been like so far at my work."

"Not really."

"Close to chaos. Lots of overtime, lots of news changing right on deadline, late nights, long shifts–you know, Hippies and the anti-Vietnam stuff, big draft card burnings in Golden Gate Park, the protest marches downtown and in Berkeley and Oakland, that huge Tet Offensive in 'Nam just a little before Laura's accident. By the time I went back to work after her memorial service even Walter Cronkite was saying the war was lost."

"Yeah, I heard about that."

"Then LBJ announced he wasn't going to run again, and only four, or five, days later Dr. King was shot in Memphis and the riots began everywhere. Now, just last week in New York, the huge student sit-ins at Columbia. "Really big news just keeps coming. It'll have to level off soon."

Misty rested both elbows on the table and her chin on her clasped hands and surprised me by asking, 'Do you think Bobby Kennedy will win next month?"

"In California? Sure! In fact, he's probably going to be president. It was no surprise he didn't take the Oregon primary. But, what do you think?"

She toyed with the pepper mill. "I don't vote, but I guess I hope so. At least he's not real old. I don't much like Hippies–too dirty–but they're right about one thing, anyway–don't trust anyone over 30!"

"That lets me out," I told her. "I'm 31."

She got up, came around the table and gave me a kiss on the forehead. "You're different." she said. "You'll be good 'till you're 50. Do you mind if I take a shower? I want to put on one of my new dresses."

5.

I went out to the garage to clean the bugs off of the Porsche windshield. At work recently, I'd trimmed a wire story that said swarms of bugs were diminishing over time and people were noticing because cars no longer collected so many. When I read that, I remembered my dad hosing and scrubbing dozens of yellow ones off of the windshield and grill of our blue Dodge when I was a kid, so it sounded right. The scientists in the story appeared to think that losing insects was a bad omen, but I could've done with fewer today; this must be bug season.

Waiting for Misty and trying not to be too eager for the night ahead, I looked over the stuff on the garage shelves that ran along the side wall beyond the empty space for a second car: cleaning supplies, camping gear, two heavy paper bags full of charcoal briquettes, a round little portable barbecue pan with a tripod to set it on–we could use that for the steaks. A rake, hoe and shovel hung from a rack. I couldn't see that this place needed much gardening, but the tools gave me a thought: 'Funny that I'd told myself Misty was dressed to look like a farmer's daughter, that sexy girl in all the traveling salesman jokes. In fact, she really was a farmer's daughter, and sexy enough to be the girl in the jokes too.

I followed a narrow sidewalk around the side of the house to the front and stood on the deck to stretch after the day's drive. Most mornings I took a run, but I'd missed today. I surveyed the empty beach again. Beside the house, on my left, was the grove of eucalyptus trees, with the big pieces of bark they had shed lying under them. To the right there were only dunes, half covered with wild ice plant, part of Monterey State Beach, where the city limits ended. From the parking area, it took a hike over the dunes to reach that beach, but it might have been busier today if the water weren't so cold–not a soul in sight now.

In the house, I started setting out things to cook, put two potatoes in the oven to bake and seasoned two boneless New York steaks. Just outside the open garage door, I set up that little tripod barbecue and used a squirt of lighter fluid to fire up some charcoal briquettes.

When Misty came back out, she was wearing the white, purple and yellow floral dress and looking like Spring itself, and I told her so. She said, "Thank you!" struck a pose, and spun around so I could watch the light skirt flare out.

With the charcoal heating, we went back to the kitchen and I put together a salad, while Misty played with the dimmer switches and giggled. There were three light tracks on the kitchen ceiling, and three dimmer knobs side by side on the switch plate, so she could shift the light up and down around the room.

"A kitchen with mood lighting!" she said. "'Never saw *that* before."

I had just found candles and stubby candleholders in a drawer. "I'll show you mood lighting" I told her and set them out on the table.

She rubbed up against me like a cat. "Mmm, that'll be nice," she said and then darted away.

The coals were glowing when we took the steaks off the little grill. It was just beginning to grow dark outside. Back in the kitchen, Misty turned the track lights all the way off and I lit the candles and held the chair that faced the bay for her.

As we ate, I tried to flirt a little: "I saw you put away all your sand dabs at lunch. How do you keep such a tiny waist?"

"Are you kidding? I dance all night! You're the one who should be fat. You sit at a desk all night."

"Ah, but I run just about every sunny morning."

"You run up and down hills?"

"Nope. Most days I cheat. Our... My apartment is just around the corner from the cable car on Mason, so I take that down to the Fisherman's Wharf turntable, and then run east to the Embarcadero, then past the wharves almost to the Ferry Building and back–flat all the way. Sometimes I even walk back uphill, but I don't try to run it."

While we finished the bottle of wine and started a second, we talked across the table for most of an hour, deliciously delaying what was to come. I asked her about her life in Nebraska, and if she ever missed it. "Not for a minute!" she said. Listening to her describe it, it was easy to see why that was. Her friends were farm animals, the hunting dog and two barn cats. She missed those sometimes, but that was all. A girl needs a mother, I thought, and she hadn't had one.

The first time she'd really come across approval, it became clear to me, it was from boys in her freshman class. She'd apparently tried to make friends with some of the girls, but there was a barrier between 'town girls' and 'farm girls,' who went home on the bus after school. That barrier did nothing to stop the boys–they were all over her. So girls were rivals, and men (even now, I thought, when they put their dollars on the stage for her) were proof of her own worth.

Misty probed my life too, maybe just to be polite.

"Isn't it boring to sit at a desk all night, when you used to be a reporter?"

"Not at all. Reporting isn't like the movies; it can be boring itself. You have to wait in the hall for an hour or more to question guys when they come out of a meeting, or you get sent to cover the annual flower show and have to make a story out of that, and the next year you might get sent to cover the same show all over again. Well, on the copy desk you have to edit those stories too, but you get all the big news in the world. When wars start, or queens get married, or President Kennedy got shot, those are wire stories or stories from our own bureaus, and they go straight to the desk for us to edit. Those are breaking stories, with new facts coming in all the time, and banner headlines to write and to rewrite between editions as the story changes. There are some routine days, sure, but not that many this year."

When we'd cleared the table and put the dishes in the sink, Misty refilled my wine glass with the rest of the second bottle and poured some of Scott's Chivas Regal into a glass for herself at the wet bar, took a sip, and set both glasses down beside the telephone on the low table next to the big leather chair. She perched on its arm. "Let's sit here," she said. The light outside had faded, so the room's soft glow came only from the candles still burning on the dining table.

I sat, and Misty snuggled in beside me with her warm, pale legs across mine. I gave her a kiss on the forehead, and she turned her face up to me and took my face in her hands for a long kiss that was sexy, but something else–it felt like coming home to warmth and a hug. I'd been sorry for Misty, but I hadn't realized until then how much I missed affection myself.

"Dan, do you really think I'm pretty?" She searched my face and seemed to bite her lip. Perhaps she was more insecure than I thought; maybe she knew that her looks wouldn't last forever. I was sorry that she seemed to need an answer.

"Misty, I've been saying that all day. You're a knockout. When you dance, men put dollars down all night, so you'll come closer, just because you're a knockout–and you know that, right?"

"But all men aren't the same–do *you* think I'm pretty?" I searched her pensive face. She had some very light freckles I hadn't noticed before; maybe she'd put on less makeup after her shower.

"Yes, Misty, I think you're *very* pretty. I personally think so. What do you mean 'all men aren't the same?' I thought you told me they were."

"No there are two kinds–assholes and gentlemen. Leroy was an asshole, and there are lots more of those–but you're a gentleman."

"Maybe, but right now I don't want to be *too much* of a gentleman." I stroked her warm thigh through the silky new dress as I said it. She laughed softly, licked her lips and we kissed again. She smelled of Chivas Regal, cigarette smoke and perfume; I hadn't smelled perfume up that close or tasted lips that moist for a long time. I was short of breath.

"Besides," she said, "not all gentlemen are good looking, but you are."

"Well, it's too bad you didn't meet Scott. People at his parties say we look like brothers. But with my horn rims, I look like the schoolteacher brother, and with his Ray-Bans, he looks like the yacht captain."

"Um-hum, but you're the one I did meet, baby."

You bet I was. The anticipation I felt wedged against her in that big chair made me think of the first time with Laura, when, as college seniors, we'd made love at midnight on a couch in a faculty lounge where we didn't belong. So this was all going where I wanted, and too late to turn back.

Well, that was where I was wrong.

Misty's left hand began to trail down across my chest to my belt and what I suddenly began to feel was... unready. There's a reaction that men know, and it just wasn't happening. What I felt instead was an uncertainty that became a kind of private panic. For a moment, I'd thought maybe I even *loved* Misty, but now I couldn't seem to *want* her the way I had intended ever since Los Gatos.

Misty sensed it; her eyes were wary. "What's wrong?" she asked.

"I don't know–it's just–maybe it's still too soon after.... I didn't think so, but–"

"Come on, baby, want me to help a little?'

"No! Uh, I mean, uh, I don't think I'm...." I had said "No!" too vehemently, a bad mistake.

But Misty was still cooing. "Well what if we try..." She began to shift herself from her spot beside me. She seemed to be getting up. All my life I'd been taught to open car doors for women politely, lift grocery sacks for them, offer them a hand–so I tried to help Misty now.

"Stop!" she hissed. "Don't you push me away! "Nobody pushes me aw–"

"I wasn't!"

"Not much!"

"I just–"

"Well, swell! I know all about guys who turn you on just so they can turn you *off*!"

"That's not what–"

"–Guys who rather dump a girl than admit they're *afraid* of being close for even ten minutes!"

She was standing now with five feet between us, looking down at me, still in the chair.

"You know what? I take it back! You and Leroy are *both* assholes!"

"Hey, that's not at all what–"

Her voice was rising, "He took my money–you took my time. I could be halfway to L.A. right now–with somebody who doesn't pretend he owns a Porsche!"

"I never–"

"Look, asshole! I'll tell you what." She pointed toward the bedroom. "I'm going to sleep in there, and you're going to sleep out here! And tomorrow morning you are going to make us breakfast and drive me to the station in time for the train. So find out when it comes!" She turned to the door and shook her shoulders as to throw me off, even though I was still off balance in the big leather chair. The door slammed behind her, then after a moment opened part way, and her slender hand dropped my gym bag with a soft thump in the big room.

I hadn't seen any sign of that quick temper before, and I was upset and angry, but mostly at myself–mortified. I had humiliated myself. I dreaded having to face her in the morning. Still, she had no right to give me orders. It would be a relief to drop her in Salinas. If I was ashamed, she'd shamed me more than I deserved. Good riddance!

I didn't want to be seen by Misty, or anyone else, that night, so I struggled to my feet, pawed my way into the big coat closet, found two jackets on hangers, grabbed one, went straight to the patio door and slipped out to hike down the beach.

6.

There was no moon, and the night was growing darker still. The beach was wide now–ebb tide–again no sign of anyone on the sand. Feeling angry, frustrated and miserable, I trudged along the hard sand just beyond the lapping surf. Heading toward the distant lights of the Monterey pier downtown, I passed the comforting darkness of the eucalyptus grove and came to the community of small cottages built on the dunes. I'd walked this beach in daylight with Laura and Scott, so I knew that most of the houses were stucco or shiplap, painted in cheerful pastels, but now they were just darkened shapes with an occasional glow through a curtained window. Still, a few looked like smaller versions of Scott's house, with walls of glass facing the sea, and the two lighted ones looked like distant show windows. In one halfway up the hill I could make out a group around the table–not eating, perhaps playing some board game. In another, closer, it looked as if a couple were having a candlelight dinner. I wished them better luck than I'd had.

I didn't intend to walk all the way to restaurant row on the pier, and I knew that it was almost out of reach anyway; you'd have to detour around the Naval Post Graduate School next to the beach, halfway to town. I just wanted a place that was as lonely as I felt at the moment.

A little way past the last cluster of homes on the dunes I came to a pair of one-man sailboats that lay tipped at an angle, their sails furled, centerboards drawn up, masts pointing at stars near the horizon. In the soft breeze, the fabric covers on their cockpits lifted and fell slowly, as if the boats were breathing in their sleep. I sat down between them, trying to drop out of sight, still humiliated, angry with myself and worried.

That had never been a problem before. Perhaps there had been too little time since Laura's death–14 or 15 weeks–to think of going to bed any way but alone. But what had Scott told me? "Death is the end, but life goes on. It's normal to be sad, but don't forget you are a survivor, and survivors need to live."

It could be, though, that it was too soon to live that way yet.

Whatever our problems, Laura and I had gone back a lot longer than we'd been married–it was almost 12 years since we met as kids at the freshman mixer at Arizona State. You don't get over 12 years overnight.

Laura was in fine arts; I was in journalism–it was love at first sight for me, and it was clear that she was happy enough to have me as a reliable date. Still, we'd gone–almost–through college without sleeping together, mainly because The Pill wasn't really available much until a couple of years after we finished college.

But alone as I was now, I hated the idea that I'd have to wait longer than I already had to be close to someone again. Until I'd messed it up, it had felt so right to have Misty's warmth next to me and feel her breath on my neck–there was every reason to want that. Why hadn't I been ready for more?

Did I feel there was something just morally wrong about it–that I was disrespecting my late wife? That was possible, but I didn't like the idea or see why it should be true.

Scott had given me that "Living with a Loss" book and he must've been expecting me to be reading it and meditating alone, so maybe I felt guilty for dropping his plan so quickly? If so, I resented it.

Misty had suggested both that I was *afraid* of being close and that maybe I *enjoyed* frustrating partners. Those couldn't *both* be true, could they? Anyway, they were just wrong.

Laura was my age and all the girls I'd dated in high school were about my age too. Maybe I'd suddenly felt that I was taking advantage of a dancer six or seven years younger than I was?

Or, could it be that Misty's hint about being abused by her brother was a turnoff, so I felt sorrier for her than attracted? That didn't seem likely; I *was* sorry for her, but I'd sure as hell been attracted all day.

Possibly, I could have felt too much *like* her abusive brother after I understood what he'd probably been up to. No–too creepy to be right.

Maybe knowing how easily she could maneuver men into parting with their cash–and I'd done that today myself–made me feel manipulated and not in control.

Or–maybe I just had an embarrassing new physical problem that I didn't want to think about now.

But probably, though I didn't like that idea much either, my first thought was more or less right: it was just too soon after Laura's death and, when I thought of Laura at the wrong moment, my damn conscience got in the way.

I ran those ideas and others, back and forth for more than an hour, finally deciding I'd have to live with the last one, until, looking far down the beach, I saw that the lights on the pier were growing dim. A fog bank was stealing into the bay. There were still stars over my head, but none to see out over the ocean. I felt the cold more deeply now, zipped Scott's Levi jacket up, stood, turned and jogged back silently on the hard, wet sand toward Scott's deck, trying to put my problems behind me, unaware that I was running toward them.

7.

The candles on the table had burned down and gone out–careless to have left them burning. There was no light under the door to Misty's room and the last thing I wanted to do was face her again that night. Without turning on any lights, I could see my way around enough to find my gym bag and the door to the bath. In there, with the light on, I took a washcloth bath, brushed my teeth and got into the pajamas I'd brought before I thought about blankets for the couch. By morning it would be colder. I expected to find extra blankets in the walk-in closet, but I was wrong–if there were any, they must be kept in the bedroom closet only. I had seen a sleeping bag on the shelf in the garage earlier, so I switched off the bath light and felt my way in the dark out to the laundry room. There I flipped the wall switch for the single light bulb that hung on a cord from the ceiling. The washer and dryer looked fairly new, but the builder hadn't wasted any expense on this service porch–that's what everyone called such rooms when I was young.

In the garage, the light from the laundry room was enough to show me that I had left the garage door up. I pressed a button on the wall beside me; a weak light went on and the door rolled down with a thump that made me uneasy because it might wake Misty. I could go without another confrontation with her right now. In my bare feet I stole across the cold concrete floor to the shelves. The sleeping bag was one of the new lightweight ones, filled with down and called mummy bags because of their shape, more than I would need to be warm. Back in the big room, I carried it to the couch in the dark, opened the zipper down the front, spread it out and wriggled into it with a lot of effort but as quietly as I could. "I won't be able to sleep," I thought, but for a little while I did. Alone.

* * *

Soon after 6 a.m. I was shaving in the lighted bathroom under a skylight that showed only gray fog overhead. Once I was awake there was no point in staying on the couch; I knew I wouldn't sleep again until I'd taken Misty to the train. Maybe I'd have a nap in the afternoon.

Although I needed to call Salinas to find out what time the train would be stopping there, I was reluctant to call too soon. If I woke Misty, I'd just have to deal with her that much longer.

I was hungry, so I went to the refrigerator for a look. The big living-dining room-kitchen wasn't very cheerful this morning with no hint of sun, and with fog the color of granite against the glass. In the far corner, next to the window, a handsome black spyglass, mounted on a wooden tripod, faced the bay, but it was useless today. If you looked through it now you could have seen about eight inches, to the wall of windows.

I found the can of frozen orange juice we'd bought, opened it and spooned some into a plastic glass, added water and stirred it, all as quietly as possible. But reaching for the frozen juice can to put back in the fridge for later, I knocked the plastic glass off the counter. It clattered to the Spanish tile floor, making a mess and enough noise to wake the dead. I swore under my breath and reached for a roll of paper towels. It took a big share of them to clean up and I had to run more water, so I thought, "What the hell, she's probably awake now; It's time to call Southern Pacific."

As it happened, the southbound Coast Daylight was due

to go through Salinas at 9:40 that Sunday–earlier than I would have thought. The station master said that's when it was scheduled, and it had left San Francisco on time.

Misty still hadn't stirred that I could tell. While we had time to make a quick breakfast, driving to Salinas would take us lots longer if the fog reached that far inland, so I'd have to wake her now. I went to the bedroom door and knocked softly. There was no answer. A sudden thought hit me: What if she wasn't there? What if she had decided to take off last night? I hadn't been in the garage this morning, so I didn't even know if the Porsche was gone. I reached into my pocket and felt Scott's key ring for reassurance, but maybe he would keep a second set of keys somewhere in the house.

Without waiting, I turned the knob and went into the bedroom, dark and shadowy because of the fog, and was relieved to see that Misty was lying under a wool blanket pulled up over her head. I went to the bed, leaned over it and said, "Misty, time to get up. Time to get ready for the train."

But she didn't stir, and I got a cold chill. Something was not right. I gave the covers a yank and jumped back, horrified. Misty was on her left side, naked except for the bikini pants she'd slept in. There was a dried red-brown stain on the sheet, a small spot in her brown hair and an ugly mess between the other side of her head and the mattress.

I bolted out of there, rushed into the bathroom next door and was violently sick over the toilet. How could it be? She'd been a spitfire the last time I saw her, full of life and indignation. But now–and how about my own life now–Oh, God!

I flushed the toilet, rinsed my mouth, washed my hands

with soap and warm water and crept back to touch her leg. Cold. She'd been dead all night.

I pulled the sheet and blanket back up as they had been when I found her–covered her face–left that darkened room and closed the door softly but made sure I heard it latch. Then I sat in the big chair next to the phone–and realized that I had the shakes.

Who could have done this? Had her no-good boyfriend–Leroy–had he followed us here? Absurd! There was really no chance that Misty had been tracked to this house, and no chance she would have been here at all if I hadn't invited her to come with me–*bribed* her, really with food and clothes and the promise of a train ticket. So whatever had happened to her, looked at in the worst way, I was responsible. But what *had* happened? Someone had come into the house–and probably through the patio door that I left unlatched while I moped on the beach last night. So, burglary? But was anything missing? And even in a bungled burglary, why shoot a sleeping victim?

I slouched in the leather chair we had shared the night before and studied the blank expanse of fog across the wide glass wall, trying to find my way.

Without a social security card or driver's license, without any other scrap of ID, I could see no way to trace her. She called herself Misty, but that was a stage name, not something people were likely to name a baby girl in Nebraska in the 1940s. Doris or Joan or Mary Jean maybe, but Misty?

Mindlessly, I took a moment to make a litany of the likely working names of the girls in topless bars: Candice, Candy, Misty, Sandy, Debbie, Dolly, Brenda, Brandy–sexy-friendly names–a far cry from the old warriors, the strippers whose theater posters I remembered seeing in the City Hall press room: Tempest Storm, Lotta Ginger, Helen Bed.

Misty.

It was a wisp of a name–nothing to hold, nothing to see, a name for the fog that lay up against the windows of the beach house. Well, the police could do what I knew they had done with others–take a photo of her today, airbrush it to hide the blood, paint her eyes open, make a photographic copy and show it around the topless clubs in the city like any other black and white snapshot until someone named her....if anyone knew her real name. It was up to the police now. Reluctantly, I reached for the heavy phone on the little table beside my chair, shamefacedly rehearsing my next corny line: "Operator, I want the police!"

Then, very slowly, and without dialing zero, I put the phone back on the table. I *didn't* want the police, of course. I had to have them, but I didn't *want* them. It was going to be really embarrassing.

And worse.

I finally saw for sure how bad worse could be. When the cops arrived, who would be the prime suspect? Didn't they always focus first on whoever reported the crime? As for the list of suspects, there was me and... nobody.

I thought I knew a little about the police mind. The *Record-Courier* had a policy of sending every new reporter through two or three months on the police beat as an understudy to Jimmy Jerome, our tough-shelled old cophouse reporter. When Jimmy left you a memo, you could sometimes see he couldn't spell, but he didn't need to. He was not a writer but a legwork reporter; he knew how to interview cops; he got the facts that made it a story, and he phoned them in, usually to Emily Holm. Emily wrote it, but Jimmy Jerome got the byline.

Jimmy was the guy who taught me an invaluable lesson:

"The shorter the question, kid, the longer the answer. They can't give you yes or no if you just ask, 'And then what?'" He worked Tuesday through Saturday afternoon and evening. The new guy learned the beat with him Thursdays through Saturdays and covered Sundays and Mondays alone. But Ed Harris, the city editor, didn't like to leave new people in the cophouse too long. "You start to think like a cop," Ed told me. "Pretty soon, everybody's guilty. Reporters need the truth; detectives just need a confession."

So what chance would I have now as the only logical suspect? And for that matter what did I have for an alibi? My alibi was that I'd shared dinner and drinks with a pretty girl in a house that had only one bed, and that when she had undressed down to her panties and rolled into that bed, I got the great idea to sit alone on a cold beach for more than an hour watching fog come in. My alibi was that some unknown killer or killers had shot the girl when I was the only one in the whole world who even knew where she was. Some alibi!

Once the police heard that, they were going to book me then and there. My name on the police blotter–a matter of record. It would be *news*! How the other S.F. papers would enjoy catching the *Record* with *my* pants down! That's how it would look, at least. One of the city's papers, which used to be fairly high-toned back when I first came to town, had a new publisher now, and for its street editions it sometimes used banner headlines like "AMAZING SEX SURPRISE." It would be a cinch to write one of those for it now: "SIN BEFORE SLAUGHTER."

When that kind of stuff came out, what would the friends who had come to Laura's memorial service think of her grieving husband? What would my own pals on the copy desk think? But I might not have to face them. I'd lose my job–if I didn't go to prison. And I would go to prison–of course I would. God! For the first time in my life I needed a lawyer.

And there was Scott, too. What a pal I am. He lends me his high-priced car; I use it to pick up a woman. He lends me his weekend hideaway; I make it a murder scene–or a "slaying scene" anyway–it's libel if your paper calls it murder before the authorities call it murder. An editor has to watch that.

But they'd call it murder all right.

What had I done to my friend's life? There was a dead girl in his bedroom–would he ever be able to sleep there again? Say he wanted to sell this place now, what would a "murder house" be worth? A town this size wouldn't soon let go of a juicy story. This place would be on the scandal tour for years.

If only it hadn't happened here. If only her body wasn't in that bedroom; it made no sense anyway. If someone was out to kill her, why here? Couldn't it somehow have happened out in that fog....out in the bay. Why did the cops, of all people, have to know she was missing? Nobody else knew!

No....nobody else knew.

I sat there for a little while, turning that over.

It was still not quite 7 a.m. I got up and crept over to the glass door and the unseen bay, a picture window with no picture now, only the gloom, heavy and wet. By noon, Monterey might be sunny, but this blanket wouldn't begin to lift until 9 or 10 at least.

Once, on a warm Sunday afternoon last August, after Laura and I had driven down for the day, Scott and I had pushed his stubby little aluminum boat out through soft surf for a short row on the bay. Scott stored the boat upside down on the sand under the deck outside, chained to a redwood deck support. I remembered that before he and I could use the boat, he had taken a key to the big padlock out of the back of a shallow drawer in the kitchen. I went to look. Sure enough.... the key was there now.

I had to work fast.

8.

There was no breeze, but it was cool on the water. The oar locks gave a high, rusty whisper with each pull. The sea, slapping softly against the aluminum hull, sounded like the sloshing inside the Boy Scout canteen I'd had when I was twelve. I could hear my own labored breath, but everything else was silence. The dark sea seemed to dissolve into the heavy gray sky with no horizon line at all, a great void. I fastened my eyes on the few feet of wake I could see, hoping to row straight out, not swing in a circle, determined to get half a mile or more from the beach.

Watching the wake like that helped to keep my gaze too high to focus on the bulky shape in the sand-covered mummy bag at my feet. Still, wherever I set my eyes, I had to face her all the way out, and I knew that I might not have been able to do any of this if I hadn't brought that bag into the house the night before.

Dealing with Misty's nearly naked body had been almost too much for me, but, wearing a pair of gray work gloves from the garage, I was able to roll and half-lift her into the bag on the bed, then zip it closed. The beach at Scott's was fairly steep close to the deck and the tide was on the rise, so it wasn't too difficult to drag the boat, with its nearly flat bottom, down near the water and then half carry, half tug the sleeping bag down beside it. But once I'd lifted and lowered it into the boat I wasn't done. I needed to get the other things that were hers out of the house and add some weight to the mummy bag, so, panting, I went back one more time for her shoes, clothes and the bait box.

In the bedroom, I sorted through the green box hastily—lipsticks, rouge and eye shadow stuff in the metal tray that lifted when the lid was raised, brushes and heavier bottles and jars of perfume, shampoo, and liquid cosmetics below. But I paused over a shiny dark blue spray can with a golden top. It felt so light it might float. When I twisted the two pieces, the can came apart in my hands. It was empty and dry inside, except for a small roll of bills. I counted eight hundreds and three twenties, put them back in the can quickly, and left it on Scott's desk. I wasn't about to rob the dead, but there was no point in sinking money in the sea.

At the boat, once I had unzipped the sleeping bag all the way down, I worked Misty's shoes, clothes and bait box into the empty foot of the bag, trying hard not to think about what I was doing and, at the same time, imagining that an armed posse was ready to materialize out of the fog and surround me. Then, still wearing Scott's Levi jacket, and my shirt, pants, athletic shoes and socks, I dragged the boat into seawater. So I was already spent when I took the oars.

I tried to row easily, with a steady stroke, because if I stopped, I'd lose the wake and the boat might drift off course in the fog. Eventually, after perhaps twenty minutes that seemed far longer, I told myself that I was in deep water and rested on the oars, panting.

I don't think anyone has the right to decide that someone else is a throwaway person, even if they are a person no longer. Still, I didn't seem to have a choice. If the world learned about her death, and I was charged with it, the crime would never be solved, never be avenged. But if the world didn't know, then things could go on as before and pointless mistakes could be avoided—for me, for Scott, for the police and courts, for everyone.

It was pathetic, I thought, but there was no one to miss

her but me. She'd rejected her family and they'd apparently rejected her; she had not told me about anyone close in San Francisco except the cheat of a boyfriend who had robbed her. And she was on her way to L.A. where no one was waiting for her to arrive. If news of her death in the "society dentist's" bed came out in the papers, it might cause a flurry of interest in San Francisco, but I could still be the only one who really cared that she was gone. My heart was pounding. I had never done anything like this; I didn't want to do it now. But here I was.

I wanted to pull the fog around me tighter. It hid the boat, it hid the body, it hid my shame. And there was plenty of shame to hide. I had betrayed a friend, dishonored the memory of my own wife by planning to bed a woman whose real name I didn't even know, humiliated myself by botching the whole affair, and then left her to her fate while I went off to sulk in the night. And here I was, making excuses to cover it all up, probably sinking any chance to catch her real killer. What I most wanted the fog to hide from me was that I was even now making myself an accessory to murder.

I was no Jimmy Jerome on the police beat, but I knew this much: if you hide the body, you're part of the crime.

9.

I had been quick enough to decide that my only course was to put Misty's body into the bay, but finding the means and the courage to do that took longer. I was pretty sure the boat was now in deep water, but drifting in the fog without a wake meant that I no longer had any clue about the direction it was facing, and I saw that in any case there was no way to hold the boat in position while I was working the sleeping bag overboard; trying to shift the bag's weight would almost certainly cause the prow to swing around to another compass point. So until this heavy fog lifted, I might be rowing back to Scott's beach, across the bay toward Santa Cruz or out to the open sea.

That was a test for later; now I lifted the oars out of the water and into the boat and began to lean over the sleeping bag that lay at my feet. Just leaving the seat and crouching beside it in the aluminum hull made the craft rock some from side to side and warned me that maneuvering the bag was going to be tricky. For stability, I thought it probably helped that the boat's hull below the waterline was fairly flat, but this shallow rowboat was meant to hold no more than two bodies, and, in fact, there were two in it now. If I tried to put the sleeping bag over one side, I'd have to move to that side myself, and that could overturn us, so it was going to have to go over the square stern, and I was going to have to stay low in the boat to get it there. I crouched on the left side of the bag and tried to slide it a bit to the right to balance my own weight. The boat rocked some, but not too badly. I moved back a few inches toward the stern and tried that again where the bag was heavier. This time the boat tilted so much that some seawater, a few cups, sloshed over one side

I would have to lower the center of gravity, so I'd have to get lower myself by lying down left of the body, inching along, and shifting the bag to the right slightly to keep the weight fairly even. I tried that. It worked better, but it wasn't easy. The aluminum hull was cold, with shallow ribs to maneuver over every foot or so. My shoes, socks and lower pant legs were wet. The sand that had stuck to the bag when I dragged it across Scott's beach, now scraped my cheek and I had to keep my eyes closed to protect them. And I couldn't avoid the macabre thought that I had been hoping to lie next to Misty almost since I met her, and now, in the worst way I could imagine, I was doing just that.

Over the next minutes, I set my mind just on trying to squirm back–or aft maybe–so slowly that the boat rocked only a little, and when I felt the hard edges of the bait box through the foot of the mummy bag I knew I was where I wanted to be. I tugged the bag a bit toward the stern–the metal floor was wet and slick now, so the bag moved just a little more readily. With plenty of effort, while lying on my side I was able to lift the small end of the mummy bag up, with the heavy bait box inside, and over the stern into the water. It made a soft splash.

For a moment it seemed that things were fine. In the silence, I could hear the quiet pop of bubbles as water forced air out of the bag and box, and I assumed I would be able to keep feeding the bag over the stern as the weight of what was already in the water helped pull the rest along, Then I rose just enough in the rocking boat to open my eyes and look over the stern.

The sea was right in my face! The stern was so low that

the water was already less than an inch from flowing into the boat. With all the weight at the back like this, the prow must have risen clear of the water. If the bag slid further overboard, the boat was going to be swamped–I was about to go down with Misty, and it served me right!

In a panic, I sat up and lunged back to the top of the bag, lifted it and its stiff contents and, with one great effort, slid, pushed and almost hurled it over the stern and into the bay while the boat rocked and bounced crazily and gallons of seawater poured over the stern and the gunwales. I was on the way to my death!

But with the weight of the body gone, the boat bobbed higher in the water and stabilized. Now an inch or more of water was sloshing in the hull and there was nothing to bail with anywhere. Aching and exhausted, I crawled forward to the seat, breathing heavily and sore in both legs and arms, and leaned over the oars. As I'd expected, the prow was swinging slowly around. Bubbles about the diameter of a quarter or half dollar were still appearing, but beside the boat now, not at the stern. I watched them, too tired to do anything else. Just when I thought the stream of bubbles had stopped, a bigger one, the size of an overturned cereal bowl, came to the surface, hesitated for a moment, then popped.

It looked to me like a soul escaping.

That thought just told me that the morning's effort had left me not too far from unhinged. I needed to get a grip, so I continued to sit there in the fog, practicing slow breathing. It may be that I said a prayer for Misty's soul then too. My folks had been fairly regular churchgoers when I was a kid, but the last time I'd been in church was one Sunday morning in Army basic training, when Coleman, the tough black sergeant who ruled my platoon, had marched us all to the Base Chapel with no chance to opt out.

So I prayed for Misty, or maybe just meditated about her soul, but it seemed to help–or help me, anyway–because my first sign of any luck came when I looked up again and saw that, while the fog still wrapped everything, there was a hint of a horizon line now between the gray sky and the sea. I gave one pull with the starboard oar to rotate the boat slowly, and I thought I could see just a little more light in the fog in one direction than in the others. It was probably about 9 a.m. and the sun in early May would be in the southeast at this hour, so I would row toward that lighter area and, I hoped, toward land.

It worked. The fog continued to thin until, though I could see no details, there was faint silhouette to mark the top of the dunes in the mist. But when the sun became a pale disc and burned the fog away a little more, it was clear that I was off course by a lot, heading toward Seaside and further up the coast from downtown Monterey and the beach house than I wanted to be. Bone tired, I still had to swing right and row almost parallel to the coast for another twenty minutes as the sun began slowly to creep out. Dreading being seen on the water, I kept the shore in sight but stayed as far away as I could until I was closer to Scott's house. Then I turned straight for it, rowed with the last energy I had and did my best not to dawdle.

When, at last, the prow edged up on his beach, I stumbled out on the wet sand, still in my soaked pants and tennis shoes, and tipped the boat up on its port side to spill the seawater out. Then I dragged the boat by its prow closer to the house, went back to carry the oars up beside it, climbed the steps to the deck and collapsed.

10.

I didn't want ever to move again, but I lay on the deck less than a minute or two because it was still in the shade, and tired as I was, I was colder still. In the house I needed a blanket, but I knew now that they were kept only in the bedroom closet, so I had to go past that bed again. I found a large quilt, came back to the living room with it wrapped around me, and settled into the big chair, shivering. It didn't take me long to realize that what I needed most was a hot shower–my feet were never going to warm up any other way, so I ran water into the bathroom basin until it was hot, then adjusted the shower and stayed in it for a while, savoring the heat on my sore back and washing the sea-salt away. Dressing, I switched to dry underwear and a clean polo shirt from my bag, but for a two-night stay I had brought just the dark grey twill pants I'd been wearing, and they needed to be washed and dried, along with Scott's Levi jacket, so I had to borrow from his closet. I didn't want to put on his dress clothes and the only casual things there were sandals and a pair of khaki shorts; those would have to do.

Ever since I outgrew them at age eight, I had refused to wear short pants. Long pants meant you were grown up; short pants were for little kids. I had never put that idea aside, not even now. In grammar school–not at recess, but on the way home when there were no teachers around–big kids might pick on you. "Hey, shorty pants!" three of them would yell, "We're going to pants you!" You had to run or fight, and you knew you'd lose either way. Since when, in the history of mankind, had seven-year-olds ever triumphed over nine-year-olds? Nowadays, though I told myself I didn't really care what others wore, and though every year there seemed to be more grown men choosing to wear shorts in public, it still disturbed me a little when I saw a 45-year-old tourist dressed like that in the lobby of a San Francisco hotel or bank. He was asking for trouble.

The hot shower had restored me some, but I still felt weak, and I realized that I was starved. I'd had no breakfast and, when I first found Misty dead, I'd lost most of my dinner–all before that long row on the bay. Now it was past noon, but I started by making coffee, using a spoon to eat the remaining frozen orange juice concentrate, thick and sweet, right out of its cardboard can, and making toast. Then I put together an omelet, frying and crumbling up crisp chunks of the bacon we'd bought. I ate the first half of the breakfast standing at the stove while cooking the rest, but I finished on a stool at the counter, munching an apple with my second mug of hot coffee while I made a mental list of the cover-up tasks still to do.

What I really wanted right now was just to hop into the Porsche and drive back to San Francisco as fast as I dared without attracting attention. I sure didn't want to hang around waiting to see if the killers decided to come back, but going now would leave a house full of evidence for the Monterey Police. No, when I got out of here later today, I needed to leave no trace that I had been in Monterey at all, and no sign of a crime in this house.

Both the dinner dishes and those from my late breakfast were still in the sink, but there were more important places to begin.

First came the bed. Even if I had to tell everything to Scott, I didn't want him to have to walk into his own house and find that mess. So I had to start in the bedroom. I began by stripping the sheets, dried blood and a bullet hole in each, and putting them into the washer on cold water wash with bleach because I knew hot water would set the stains. When the blood was gone, I'd put them through again with soap and hot water. Carrying physical evidence of a murder through the house made it real all over again. Somebody had done it–possibly by mistake–but how and why? And who? And would they be back?

I went to work in earnest. The sooner all the evidence was gone, the sooner I could disappear. There was a bullet hole in the single woolen blanket on the bed, with a stain about the size of a silver dollar around it. I soaked the stain in cold water at the bathroom basin, then soaped and rinsed it and squeezed as dry as I could, and draped the damp part over the desk chair in the sun from the clearstory windows.

The queen-sized mattress had a brown-red stain too large to erase. It was hard trying to balance and flip the mattress by myself, but, after it went over, with the other side up, it looked innocent enough, and it was a relief to see it that way. Of course it would have to be replaced later, but for now that was the best I could do. I got another set of sheets from the closet, and made the bed as if for a guest, leaving the blanket on the chair to dry and put back later. Misty's empty spray can with her stash of bills was still on Scott's small desk. I stuck it in my gym bag for safe keeping, just because there was no other way to hide it and hold on to it. I wasn't even willing to pay myself out of it for the clothes I'd bought her when I thought she was almost broke–they had been a gift, and anyway, they were already gone. She had never even gotten to wear the red striped dress.

The more I worked, the sorrier I felt for Misty, the guiltier I felt about abetting a murderer and the more fearful I became about being caught.

My tennis shoes were starting to dry a little on the now-sunny deck as I went back for the rowboat. I stored it, again upside down and with the oars under it, beneath the deck, used the chain and padlock to fasten it to the deck support, and returned the key to the back of the kitchen drawer. The washer's spin ended, and I reset the control for hot water to put the sheets through a second cycle.

Then I went through the house room by room looking for clues the cops would find if, for some reason, they were led here. At the wet bar, a glass ashtray on the counter held three snuffed-out cigarettes marked with tell-tale lipstick, perhaps Misty's last traces. It made me unhappy to see them, but I didn't hesitate; I flushed them down the toilet and washed the ashtray in the basin.

Except for my shoes, and my wet clothes waiting their turn in the washer and dryer, everything I had brought with me, I thought, was in my gym bag now–even my billfold with about fifty remaining dollars.

In the kitchen again, I opened the refrigerator. Anyone could have bought the stuff there. I'd eat some of it for a quick Sunday supper just before I left, use up the fresh vegetables in a salad, maybe, grill some of the hamburger and ditch the rest. The bottled stuff would keep. But as I glanced at the bottles in the door rack, I got a new jolt. A catsup bottle there had a white label, and on that label someone had left part of a thumbprint in red catsup. Fingerprints! This one wasn't mine–we hadn't used catsup–but the house would be full of fingerprints that were mine, and full of Misty's too.

So I found a dry dish towel and started wiping down just about everything, starting with the telephone and the glass ashtray I'd just put back in the wet bar.

Then, wearing rubber gloves I found under the sink, I worked fast to wash and dry dishes, polishing glasses and plates more thoroughly than I would have otherwise. The washer stopped and I moved sheets to the dryer and put my own clothes at last into the washer. Still wearing the rubber gloves, I went out to wipe the steering wheel and other surfaces of the Porsche. When I put the garage door up for more light, the first thing I saw, just outside, was the little three-legged barbecue grill we had used, with its dead grey ashes. I had left it out on purpose last night because the coals were still warm, and it seemed safer to keep it outside. Now I could use it for supper again. But, walking around the rear of the car to look at it, I saw something else–something that made me consider my situation in a new light altogether.

11.

Just beyond the far side of the garage, standing alone on the asphalt and near the door that led to the bedroom, was a big gasoline can, the kind I knew well from my days in the Army–an olive drab, tall rectangular 5-gallon metal can with one angled corner where the cap sat. The Army still used them, so far as I knew, but nowadays those cans often sold as well at army surplus stores. This one hadn't been there when we drove in yesterday, or when I was barbecuing on the asphalt apron just outside the garage before dinner–I couldn't have missed seeing it.

I went over to it reluctantly, more and more uneasy. It sat just eight feet from the door to Scott's bedroom, the room where Misty had been shot.

Suddenly I saw it all. Arson! Someone had planned to kill Scott–not Misty–and set a fire to hide the crime. Of course they hadn't been after Misty. It was Scott who was often here on weekends and Scott's car was in the garage now. Neither Misty nor I was expected here last night and neither of us by any stretch of the imagination had enemies so intent on erasing us that they'd burn down a house just to make sure. This looked like it could be retribution for something. Or maybe someone was in debt to Scott a lot more than they intended to pay. Whatever it was, they wanted Scott dead, but they had really messed up, and now Misty was gone, and it was my mistake that she was at the bottom of the bay. I was still an accomplice. There was nothing good about that olive-drab can. Wearing the rubber gloves, I jarred it by the handle a little. It was full or close to it, and I knew from my Army days that those cans could weigh 40 pounds or more loaded–a pretty heavy lift. The assassins must have bugged out in a hurry when they pulled back the covers and found they'd shot someone they didn't know, and the can was probably too bulky to take with them. I tried the lock to the back door. The knob turned easily, and when I pushed gently, the door started to open, so there was no deadbolt. I closed the door again quickly. Scott needed to be warned!

I went through the garage to the phone in the living room, tried to dial–that's hard to do in rubber gloves, I learned–pulled the gloves off and called Scott's apartment on Russian Hill. Seven rings–no answer. He'd traded the Porsche for my station wagon because he had boxes to haul out of the office, so maybe he was there doing that. I called information, got his office number, which I'd never needed to memorize, and tried that one.

A woman's voice with what sounded like a hint of New York in it answered: "Dr. Croswell's office."

"Does Dr. Croswell happen to be there right now?"

"This is the answering service. He'll be checking in later today; you wanna leave a message?"

"How often does he check with you?"

"At least twice a day on weekends–next time late afternoon, usually."

"Okay. Would you just ask him to call his best friend at his house in Monterey right away? Please give him this call first and tell him it's very important!"

"Call best friend, Monterey house, right now, got it."

I thanked her, hung up, put on the gloves and wiped the phone again, though I was beginning to doubt that destroying my traces was important. Maybe Scott and I were both going to have to be calling the Monterey Police here anyway.

I still did not like waiting around to see if assassins showed up again, but I had no other way to take Scott's call and I didn't know how else to reach him. Much as I would like to be home, or anywhere but here, I'd stay to get the laundry dry and out of sight. And, starting now, I'd look for any clue to explain why Scott was a target.

Nothing in the kitchen drawers told me anything, nothing in the big room seemed to be a hiding place. A blond bookcase stood against the wall between the doors to the bath and bedroom, full mostly of classics and fairly recent best sellers like "Catch 22." There was no way I was going to shake out every book to see if something was hidden there. In the bedroom, the little desk had a tier of drawers on the right-hand side. The drawer above the kneehole held pens, pencils, scissors, a letter-opener and a checkbook from the Monterey Branch of Wells Fargo. It showed a balance of only $214, but most of the check stubs listed small, amounts for groceries or utilities or such. Scott's main bank would be in San Francisco. Among the letters in the back of that drawer were one from the power company requesting payment and one from the phone company warning that service would be suspended if an overdue bill wasn't paid. But the letters were several months old, the lights were still on and I'd just used the phone, so Scott had probably paid in person. Easy to overlook bills when you didn't always live where they come due, I thought.

The next drawer held only plain paper, envelopes, mailing labels and stuff of that sort, but in the deep file drawer below I did find something of a surprise. There were Xeroxed copies of real estate closing papers showing that Scott Croswell had sold this property to Monterey Peninsula Rentals Ltd. four years ago, in June. And the file just behind it held monthly rent receipts to the same company going back that far. Occasionally a month was missing, and the next payment was for two months and a late penalty. Scott Croswell was renting the beach house he had once owned, and he'd occasionally been hit and miss about payments. Perhaps he wasn't as well off as I'd always assumed, so that was a possible sign of financial trouble. On the other hand, you don't burn a house down over a late phone bill or a try to shoot a renter over a missed payment. I was not even close to a motive.

12.

Scott's call came at 6:30. By that time I had folded the dry sheets with the bullet holes, looking like nothing more than moth holes now, deep inside. And I'd replaced them in the closet, putting my own clothes and Scott's jacket in the dryer.

I flinched when the phone rang and had to clear my throat before I picked up. Having to tell my friend what a mess I had made of this weekend was a nasty thing to face.

Because the call was long distance, there was always a chance that an operator could be listening in, so I had rehearsed what to say: "Scott, there has been real trouble at the house, and I think you need to drive here now. Do you know of anyone who could be an enemy? I don't want to talk on the phone. When can you get here?"

"Hey, Killer, is it really that urgent?"

"Yes, Scott, I really think it is! Maybe life and death–I just don't want to say any more on the phone."

Scott sounded out of sorts. "Look, I've got a dinner date in half an hour and it's too late to cancel. I'll have to cut it short, but I can't start down there till at least 8:30 or so. That means I ought to be there about 10:30 or later."

"Okay, that'll work–It'll have to." We hung up. Scott was annoyed, but he didn't know what I knew. And I was annoyed too–now that I was going to spill everything to him, I wanted to get it over with, but there were four hours to wait, in a house where there had been a murder last night.

At least it was still light at this hour, and windless, and

because I'd had only breakfast today–or maybe it was a Sunday brunch–I was hungry. So I took the hamburger out of the fridge to let it warm and used lighter fluid again to start new charcoal briquets burning on the ashes of last night's cooking. While I waited for the grill to heat, I made myself a small salad and wrapped a baking potato in aluminum foil to cook outdoors–last night the little grill had had only room for two steaks. Then I went out to the deck to bring in my nearly dry shoes.

There was going to be a magnificent Pacific sunset–you could tell already. The banks of cumulus and stretches of high cirrus clouds that had started gathering after the fog lifted were still only wan pastels–light pinks and lavenders, but as the sun dropped lower behind them, they would become reds and golds and shades of lavender and perhaps even some light turquoise, an over-the-top display of California excess. I'd have a glass of wine and the salad now at the dining table where I could watch, so I went out to put the potato on the grill above glowing coals.

At dinner last night I had taken the chair facing the kitchen, so that when Misty sat across from me, she could see the bay in the fading light. But now I sat where she had, to watch the sky turn brilliant while I sipped red wine. When the show was at its best, I got up and went out on the deck for a moment just to see more of the sky. A three-word sentence I'd heard there recently came to me and I said aloud without thinking: "It beats Nebraska."

Instantly, my own view of the sunset went from Technicolor to black-and-white. Misty had deserved to see this, and I'd been sitting in her chair, watching it happen by myself, all the while looking toward the bay where, thanks to me, she was lying somewhere–no telling where–in the dark. I had never felt more ashamed.

The only remedy was to keep busy. I took a plate and

went through the garage to cook the burger and tend the potato, reminding myself again that, even if I had brought her here, I hadn't caused Misty's death. By mistake I had involved myself, made it my murder, but her killing had nothing to do with me.

I had lost my appetite, but I ate anyway, sitting now at the counter where I'd had breakfast, while the clouds lost color and the sky turned gray, then black. When I finished, I went ahead with trying to erase any sign that I had ever been here by washing and polishing the dishes I had just used, cleaning the coffee pot and checking the dryer. My clothes were dry, but my dark gray pants were wrinkled.

It was just about nine. I had plenty of time before Scott would arrive and with all I had to confess, I didn't want him to find me wearing his damned short pants. There was a portable ironing board leaning against the wall in the narrow space next to the dryer; I pulled it out and set it up under the hanging bulb in the center of the little room, got a steam iron out of the cupboard above the dryer, filled it in the kitchen, let it heat and went to work.

I had just begun when I was both relieved and unsettled to hear what sounded like my own Ford pull up somewhere on the asphalt outside. If it was Scott, he was so early he must have decided to ditch his date after all. Maybe what I'd said about "life and death" had jarred his curiosity. But when no one came in for more than two minutes I kept ironing, thinking I'd been wrong and might as well finish. Just then the door to the garage opened and Scott appeared, slouching casually against the jam.

"Well, Killer, what's up?"

"Scott, it's important! Someone tried to murder you last night—I wasn't here, but a girl hitchhiker I picked up was in your bed. They shot her! She's dead!"

"Ahh—where is she now?"

"It was really foggy– I took your boat and put her way out in the bay. I'm really sorry, but you have to understand–there was no one for the cops to blame but me. I guess I panicked, but–"

Scott moved closer. "You dumped a body in the bay?"

"In your sleeping bag. I had to put her in *something*! I'll pay for the bag but if I–"

Unexpectedly, Scott gave a harsh laugh. His voice dripped contempt I'd never heard in it. "Yes, I'll definitely want compensation for the sleeping bag– you clueless moron!"

Looking up–astonished– I suddenly saw him standing right at the end of the ironing board and lifting a black pistol with a huge muzzle at me. "Well," he said, "you've cleaned up the worst of it–but you nearly ruined everything! Never mind. 'Turns out we can fix it all right now!"

I had never even seen a pistol with a silencer, but I knew I was looking at one, and, terrified, I reacted instinctively. With my left hand on the heel of the ironing board I gave the board a hard shove that drove its narrow end into Scott, just below his waist, and swung the iron in my right hand up to smash the light bulb overhead. There was a flash and the room went black. All at the same moment, as Scott roared in pain, there was a second flash and bang in the dark, then another. I don't know whether I heard the gun going off or bullets hitting the wall, but shots are shots. In the total dark, I swung the iron wildly back and forth at arm's length, hoping to knock the gun away. The ironing board went over with a crash. I *hated* Scott now without knowing why! I felt the iron connect hard with something as Scott roared again. My hand went numb, but I held on to the iron for my life! I swung again, connected again–and again. Silence. The gun had clattered to the floor somewhere. The only sound now was a ringing in my ears and my own gasping breath as I leaned on the washer, trying to listen for movement, my heart racing as I struggled to recover and understand. The faint scent of singed hair hung in the room.

I was in deep trouble now! Shocked and exhausted, I waited as my eyes began to adjust to darkness. Then, what I could dimly make out was enough to drive me out of there into the kitchen. But with that door open to shed faint light into the laundry room, the view was worse, awful, in fact. Scott's lower right arm was clearly broken, bent almost as if it had a second elbow, and his head was battered on the left side, blood pooling on the vinyl floor and spattered elsewhere. There was no chance he was alive.

I wanted to get out of there–not just out of the room where Scott was sprawled, but out of that whole jinxed house, out of Monterey! Desperate, I pulled my pants from between the wall and the overturned ironing board, retreated into the kitchen, dialed the track lights almost off, got out of the shorts and hurled them through the door in Scott's direction, and pulled on my own long pants. I grabbed my gym bag and canvas shoes–not dry, but dry enough–and dressed as fast as I could. I was ready to bolt to my Ford when I balked. I had Scott's keys, but I didn't want anything to do with his car or his stuff, and my own key ring was somewhere–probably in Scott's pants pocket. I'd had to have it, so I had to dig it out.

Still worried about fingerprints, I wiped Scott's keys with the dishtowel and tossed them into the service porch. I found the steam iron there on the floor and wiped its handle. It had come unplugged but the iron itself was still too hot to touch. Then I held my breath as I squatted beside the body–careful to keep my eyes on Scott's shoes and nothing else–and reached gingerly into his still-warm left front pocket. When I felt the keys and pulled, there was something loosely tangled with them–a door key, attached to one of the four-inch, hard plastic tags most motels used. Back in the kitchen I turned up one light over the counter to read the message engraved in white into the brown plastic: "Room 16–Postage Guaranteed. Drop in any Mailbox, Cloud Nine Motel, 87721 El Camino Real, San Mateo, CA 94005"

13.

I wanted to run but struggled for self-control. Still having trouble breathing, I surveyed the entire big room from the lighted kitchen. Nothing of mine was there. I had my wallet, my gym bag with my clothes. Wait! I had never put my razor or toiletries case back in the gym bag. They were in the bath, out of sight in the cupboard under the sink. I had stashed them there in the morning so they wouldn't be in Misty's way when she was getting ready for the train. Now I rushed into the bath and found them, shoved them into my bag and switched off lights as I left. Ready to flee, I killed the only track light still burning in the kitchen, leaving the entire house as dark as the back room had been. But I knew my way now. I pushed through that small, awful room and into the garage, dodged to my left in the dark to avoid the front end of the Porsche–and immediately sprawled over a heavy object that went down with me.

The gas can! Scott must have moved it up before he came in. Gas was spilling! I could strongly smell it and hear it slosh out–the cap was already off or very loose. Flailing out in the dark, my hand found the Porsche, then its door handle. I scooped up my gym bag, and jerked myself up against the car fast before gasoline could get on my clothes. Rattled, and with the bag in one hand, I tried to use the low-slung car body to support and guide me, but, as I leaned on it awkwardly, with my feet out behind me, my left foot briefly caught on something that felt lightweight but fell with a loud metallic crash. I finally got upright and stood behind the Porsche. Even in the dark I could tell right away what had gone over–the little tripod and the barbecue pan I'd used to cook supper. Overturning it had stirred up the coals and now some lay on the garage floor glowing. I didn't need to know more to start running.

Outside it was still dark–no moon to see–but I could make out my station wagon on the far side of the asphalt apron, and I stumbled toward it, still lugging the gym bag; Scott had parked my car close to the road and pointing away from the house, as if for a quick getaway. I yanked the door open and piled in, fumbled to work the key into the ignition, jammed down the clutch pedal, shifted into neutral, twisted the key, hit the accelerator, and was relieved to hear the engine come to life. Just as I shifted into third there was a *whoosh* like the sound of a huge pilot light catching, and the row of dark cypress trees across the road from me lit up for a second as if it were noon. In the rear-view mirror I caught a glimpse of the whole inside of the garage in one big blaze as I tore out of there and spun around the eucalyptus grove next door. I was halfway down the hill to Del Monte Boulevard before I realized that I had better turn my headlights on.

I had to pause at the street, not just for the stop sign, but for two cars coming from the right and a pickup truck from the left, so I used the time to pull myself together and the seatbelt across my lap. That helped to calm me: "Drive safely!" and I made a careful left-hand turn onto the thoroughfare, heading for home. But I was too keyed up to simply follow traffic; I had to pass whenever I got a chance.

After a couple of blocks, I was back in Seaside, the bedroom town next to Fort Ord. Del Monte Boulevard running through it was mostly commercial, with stoplights every few blocks, so it was nerve-racking to try to beat them while faking a leisurely drive. A mile or two farther,

I went through a yellow light as it turned red and almost immediately heard a siren. My heart sank but, instead of a cop on my tail, a distant fire truck was coming toward me. I pulled over like a dutiful citizen as it passed, siren blaring, already on its way no doubt to the blaze I'd just left.

At Fort Ord, there were pools of light outside each barracks building, but the highway itself grew darker. Once I was a half-mile beyond the fort's property, I found a wide spot and pulled off on the shoulder just to breathe for a while, then got out of the car to look back at the long, dark curve of the shore and a single bright speck of fire perhaps eight miles away. My left wrist hurt from my fall, but probably wasn't sprained. The house was burning, but that was all anyone could tell from here–too far and dark to see more. Drivers heading into Monterey would probably think some party was under way with a big bonfire on the beach.

Getting back into my station wagon, I saw for the first time that the back seat was down to make cargo space and that a full-sized kid's bike was lying there. I'd never seen the bike before, and I'd never seen Scott ride. If he had a bicycle, I thought, it would be a racing bike with gears. This was a one-speed with fat tires and a coaster brake. As I started to drive again, it lay on its side behind me, another Big Fact I could not explain.

14.

Now, however, there were a number of things I could explain very well– some of which I probably would have seen sooner if I had ever had a reason to doubt Scott's friendship: First, Scott was not a prince, as I had told Misty, and he was not my friend–he was a rotten son-of-a-bitch who wanted to kill me and, apparently, burn me up. He was my enemy for no good reason I could imagine, and that had to have been true for a long time; this couldn't have come along just last week.

It began to dawn on me that Scott had been going to a lot of trouble to set me up. For some reason, he apparently wanted not just to kill me, but to kill me in his own house. That was crazy! And he was the one who offered to trade cars so he could move his file boxes, but maybe there had never been any boxes; the only thing in the back now was that unexpected bike. I could see how much trouble he'd taken, but I couldn't see why.

Driving back the way Misty and I had come, I also had time now to think about how terribly unlucky she had been to meet me. When Scott came in through that bedroom back door to shoot me, she was in the bed where I should have been, so I owed my life to her quick temper and my inept attempt at romance–nothing for me to be proud of, but my good luck all the same. Still, she'd been doomed either way. What if we'd both been in that bed? My killer wouldn't have left a witness; he'd have had to shoot us both.

I suddenly thought of something else, grim but

satisfying. Just this morning early, I'd told myself that if I called the cops, Misty's real killer might never be found, nor her death avenged. Well, not even one day after she'd died, it was avenged already. I didn't give myself any medals for that. I'd been scared to death and fighting to survive, but Scott wasn't killed in revenge. He'd brought his death on himself. That was better somehow. It was karma.

But there was also something I didn't want to explain to anyone, ever. By 9:30 or so this morning, I was an accomplice to murder. By about 9:30 tonight, I was a killer. It was self-defense, sure. I had every right, but I'd killed another human being. I had to live with that.

But I didn't have to think about it right now.

So what were the other Big Facts, like the bicycle, that I had no way of knowing? One was Scott's reason for hating me so, when he pretended to be such a good friend. Another was the motel key that came from his pocket. He must have stayed at the motel already or be planning to stay there–maybe with someone else. Much as I wanted to get home and into my own bed, I'd already decided to go by the motel on the way home to learn what I could.

Scott Croswell–and his pistol with that terrifying-looking silencer–had arrived at the beach house, just after 9 o'clock. It was only 11 now, but I was already past the freshly-painted "BERRIES'" sign on the new fruit stand and descending the hill toward Los Gatos. I would look for a lighted place where I could study a map and read the address on the motel key again.

Here's something else I had just learned: when you've killed somebody and no one knows yet, you can't help feeling like a fugitive. Even if no one is hunting for you, it's hard not to think that everybody is. So the lighted main street of Los Gatos was too public for me. Two blocks over, the street was residential and quiet, with small brick houses and old trees next to the sidewalk. I parked beside the curb, where a streetlamp's light fell between trees, and got my Auto Club map out of the glove compartment. But first, atop the pile of maps and auto papers, I found a white envelope addressed "TO EVERYBODY" in all-caps printing done with a black felt pen. It was in my car, unsealed, and everybody included me, after all, so I looked inside, and it turned out that no one had a better right, because I'd apparently written the note there myself. Typewritten, it said only: "I'm sorry. I can't bear this anymore." And under that was what certainly looked like my signature. Looking closer at the two sentences, I thought they might have been typed on my Underwood at home too. If it was meant to be a suicide note, it was certainly a vague one, and if Scott had somehow typed it himself–he'd had my apartment key all weekend because it was right there on the ring with my car keys–I couldn't see the point. Surely, he knew that a suicide can't shoot himself and then throw gasoline on the bed to set fire to a house. Scott had been determined to make me his victim, but by murder and suicide both? And if my signature was a forgery, it was a good one; how could Scott get my signature on that note otherwise? I was apprehensive about getting involved any further, but I clearly needed to head for El Camino Real and the motel in San Mateo.

I knew El Camino from my reporting days, when I'd sometimes driven down it from San Francisco past the airport and through San Mateo on my way to Palo Alto to interview people at Stanford. Beyond that, there were towns with hardly a break all along that route clear to San Jose, and big motel signs in almost every town. All I wanted from the map was the shortest way to connect with El Camino from Los Gatos, which turned out to be by cutting half-way across the peninsula, through Cupertino, to a sleepy suburb called Sunnyvale.

When I got on El Camino there, even at midnight the drive north was slow, through stop lights, cross traffic and motel neon in otherwise buttoned-up towns–Mountain View, Palo Alto, Menlo Park, Redwood City–before San Mateo took its turn.

* * *

One lesson that comes clear even to the greenest reporter is that you might be able to predict a little of tomorrow's news today, but you can't guess *any* ten years out. In 1968 most people thought of the towns I was driving through just as I did then. The South Bay towns were suburbs of San Jose. The mid-Peninsula towns around Palo Alto held tracts of modern houses on the flats and bigger homes in the hills for airline pilots, bankers and Stanford professors. Just south of San Francisco were more affordable houses and apartment buildings for the city's workers. If someone had lumped all those towns together then and told us they would one day be called 'Silicon Valley,' that would really have baffled us all. They were close to the Bay, but none of them were sandy beach towns, so why "Silicon?" It simply didn't mean anything.

* * *

The Cloud Nine Motel was on the right side of the street and you couldn't miss the cloud-shaped neon sign, but first I drove straight past it, to look the place over–to "case the joint" I suppose. It was typical–two stories with an office in the front corner and parking spaces beside a line of rooms running back away from the street. An outside stairway led up to a long balcony and the second-floor doors.

I was looking for a place to make a U-turn–signs at every intersection seemed to forbid it–when I came across an all-night diner with a little parking lot, so I turned in there.

Maybe I was just putting off sneaking into somebody else's motel room, but a craving for coffee and cherry pie with ice cream came over me and in I went. If anyone could use comfort food, I could.

The place had a streamlined-from-the-Fifties look: red Naugahyde stools on chrome pedestals at the white Formica counter, behind it a large stainless-steel coffee maker with a vertical glass tube to display the color and level of the brew, booths along one wall with matching red upholstery. The lean, middle-aged counterman had thin sandy hair under a white paper cap, a lightly stained white jacket and a ruddy face with an expression that explained how disappointing life was.

"Coffee?" he asked.

"Yeah, thanks–black–and do you have cherry pie?"

"We do."

"Can you warm it up?

"Yeah–we have a toaster oven. 'You want ice cream too?"

"Yes, please. Vanilla."

"Well, nobody in here yet ever ordered hot cherry pie and *chocolate* ice cream," he said, putting me in my place. The coffee in the mug he brought was weak, but hot. I drank and tried to prepare myself for what I thought of as the "motel job" ahead of me, until the counterman returned with my warm pie and ice cream. He had an anchor tattoo on his right forearm. "Were you in the Navy?" I asked.

"Merchant Marine–World War II. We did the same stuff as Navy, but without the big guns for protection. 'You in service?"

"Army, but Germany, after Korea was long over–peacetime."

"Un-HUH!" he said, as if I'd announced I was a deserter. But he took another tack: "What about these hippie punk draft dodgers at Stanford and Berkeley–on the news again tonight. Got nothing to do but go around raising hell–stinkin' rich kids, most of 'em. The USA ought to bundle 'em up and send 'em straight into Saigon with no training or guns or boots; they'd learn lots more than they will in Berkeley!"

Hoping to change the subject, I said, "Well, I hear the college students in France have started to riot too."

"The Frogs? I didn't know that, but I don't doubt it. Hippie Frogs are probably trying to surrender even if they don't have a war!" He went back to wrap knives and forks in paper napkins, and I finished my pie and coffee and picked up the check. He met me at the register. The bill was $1.75. I gave him two bucks and left. "Nice talking to you," I said.

15.

The vacancy sign was still glowing outside the Cloud 9 Motel when I returned and there was dim light in the office, but I drove right past and back to room 16. If Scott had the key, he'd already registered and paid, and my car was the one he'd been driving. With two floors, the place must have had about 30 rooms, but–Sunday night–only eight or ten cars were in the parking spaces. Room 16 was on the ground floor, the last one at the back, darker, away from the street, and no car was parked in the spaces nearby.

With the room key in my pocket, I left the car as quietly as I could, and, using my folded handkerchief to avoid a burn, I unscrewed the weak bulb beside the door till it went out, then stood to the side in the half-dark and knocked softly.

Nothing.

I waited and listened for sounds in the room, then knocked louder. It occurred to me only then that I could have brought the Ford's tire iron for a weapon and that if Scott had a gun any accomplice in this room might also have one, but it was too late to go back. I turned the key swiftly and stepped in, pawing for a light switch. A table lamp at the window beside me went on.

The room was vacant and smelled stuffy. It looked undisturbed, except for a medium-sized leather suitcase on the bed, and a sort of thick green canvas briefcase lying next to it.

Moving quickly and feeling like a jewel thief, I got the front door closed and found a switch on a shaded reading lamp beside the double bed, then I killed the brighter lamp. The drapes had already been drawn.

The room had been refurbished fairly recently–fresh cream paint, clean tan carpet, but there was nothing homey about it. There was a bulky TV set with a large screen, probably 24 inches, on a dark chest of four drawers. Except for a San Francisco phone book and a Gideon Bible, the drawers were all empty. At the back of the room, a short hall had a shallow closet behind folding doors on one side and the door to the bath on the other. The closet was empty. I checked the shower stall warily, half expecting to meet a knife-wielding killer, but it was untouched and dry, the soap still in its little wrapper. It was pretty clear that no one had used this room, except to leave things on the bed. Scott must have been planning to sleep here tonight.

I opened the suitcase first. Scott had packed it for what looked like a business trip somewhere, silk pajamas on top, and then two very nice suits I thought I'd seen him wear, stored in a bag that folded in thirds, with flat plastic hangers so it could be hung anywhere. Below that, dress shirts and the usual array of socks and underwear, all folded to fit neatly into the space. Two black leather shoes, one in each side of the suitcase, were wrapped in white undershirts. His ties were lying flat in a special compartment inside the lid of the suitcase. All nice stuff, but something any well-off traveler might carry.

Scott, however, would never carry it again–I still didn't quite want to wrap my head around that.

I turned to the dark green briefcase–some new fabric lighter and tougher than canvas. Back in college, I'd seen professors carrying such fat bags into class, with front pockets chock full of pens, pencils and slide rules, and big compartments behind for books, lesson plans, and, presumably, newly Xeroxed copies of dreaded mid-term exams. But the contents of this bag were nothing like that. The first thing I could identify when I undid the big front flap was just another button-down shirt, and most of the space was taken by one change of casual clothes and a flat tan zip bag of toiletries. This was a bag for a passenger to keep with him when traveling.

But, behind the divider that separated the bag into two parts were several 10- by 12-inch Manila mailing envelopes. Before looking at them I tried the bag's front pockets. Bingo!

The first thing I found was a new wallet, but it wasn't Scott's; it had a GJ monogram and held nine one-hundred-dollar bills and a few ones, tens and twenties. There was a Social Security card for Gregory Johnson, no one I knew. But the driver's license–issued by the State of Indiana–cleared that up immediately. That was Gregory Johnson's too, but with a photo of Scott, looking quite a bit younger and wearing a full beard. The beard looked real to me–I'd never seen Scott like that, but it could be a photo from his salad days, when young men tried on all sorts of new identities. So, apparently, I was looking at fake ID, and there was more, including a United States Passport, with the same Gregory Johnson name and the same black and white photo of a younger Scott–even bearded, he was a handsome dog. The passport book itself looked authentic–I wondered if blank ones had been stolen somewhere in the past. Two of the back pages appeared to have been stamped by customs agents in Mexico and Costa Rica, but if the rest was phony, those stamps might be too.

About two inches above the pocket, there was a long zipper to another compartment, wide and shallow, as if to hold maps or rulers. The contents there were even more intriguing. First, there was an American Airlines ticket folder with tickets for a flight the next morning to

Philadelphia, and a connecting flight to Paris. The seats on both planes were assigned to Greg Johnson. Behind that there were three white business-sized envelopes, each holding nine $100-dollar bills. So, $2,700, and with the $900 or so in the "GJ" wallet about $3,500. In my own little gym bag I also had Misty's stash, and while I didn't intend ever to spend a penny of it, that meant that I was now in charge of over $4,000–more than two months pay for me—almost three.

Next, I opened the big Manila envelopes. The first held two tourist maps, one of the City of Paris and one of France. I unfolded them quickly on the bed, hoping for pen or pencil symbols that might be a clue to an important location, but they were unmarked. I even held them up to the light to see if there were pinpricks to mark a spot. No luck. The second envelope held two insurance policies with Continental Equity and Life of Hartford, Conn., each in a folder that carried a logo and a small etching of an imposing building with a tower, presumably the home office. I turned immediately to the back pages with notarized signatures and dates.

Scott had taken the policies out in his own name five years ago. I was going to study them, but first I'd check the remaining Manila envelope. It contained nothing but another envelope, white and business-sized, marked "coupons." Unlike the others, it was sealed, so I tore it open. There were no coupons. There were only five or six snapshots.

I looked at the first one and stood up and kicked the bed.

16.

Kicking the bed didn't give me much satisfaction, but as much as I could hope for. My chest felt hollow. My stomach ached. I sat back down under the shaded light and bitterly reviewed the snapshots, clenching my teeth so hard my jaw hurt. The one I'd seen first must have been taken by a third party because it showed Laura in a bathing suit on the deck of the beach house, and Scott in swim trunks standing behind her with his arms around her waist and smirking as if to say, *My property*! The next three were of Laura alone, first, on some casino floor, wearing a fur coat I'd never seen; next, standing in her artist's smock by an easel with one of her abstract paintings in progress and, then, smiling and sitting, with legs crossed and lots of leg showing, in a baby-doll negligee on the edge of the very bed where poor Misty had died. There were two others, both Polaroids, that I won't describe.

I felt sick. I took my glasses off and rubbed my forehead with both hands as I tried to control my anger–and some of the anger was for myself. How could I have not seen any sign of their affair when it was going on right under my nose? No wonder Scott–my concerned friend–had gone down to watch the divers with me that Saturday. I had lost Laura; he had lost his lover! He had been grieving with me, but for his own selfish reasons. Still, he seemed to recover pretty quickly–the jerk hadn't cared as much as I did!

I was furious, ashamed of being so gullible. The taste of cherry pie–but sour now–rose in my throat and I went back into the little bathroom, pulled the plastic wrapper off of the plastic glass on the sink and rinsed my mouth repeatedly. Before tonight, I never really thought I could hate anyone, but I hated Scott. And perhaps my late wife.

It wasn't until I went back to sit on the edge of the bed, that I began to see that my first impression might be wrong. The airline folder with the tickets was still lying there. So Scott had planned to shoot me and then escape to Paris before he could be found for questioning. To Paris–if you had to hide out what a nice place to do it–only the best for old Scotty! Was he really prepared to give up his whole dental business? Still, Paris seemed like an odd choice for him. While Laura had talked incessantly about going to Paris for the art, Scott had never mentioned Paris that I could.... wait a minute!

I felt a flash of insight that was another blow to the stomach. After the divers had given up, the sheriff's deputies had advised me not to bother to apply this early for even a 'provisional' death certificate because there *was no body.* When Scott Croswell had watched the divers with me that gloomy Saturday, he hadn't been grieving for Laura, but secretly laughing at me while he *revisited the scene of a crime.* Her accident must have been faked!

So....not just anger but more humiliation. I had led a memorial service for a woman who was not "resting in peace" but sleeping with my "best friend."

Laura, as I now understood things, must be waiting in Paris for her lover.

She must have flown there right after the 'fatal' Volkswagen plunge. Or maybe Scott put her on a plane first and then staged the accident. She couldn't have just hung around the Bay Area after that–someone would have seen her. And I had wasted three sad months of my life for no damn reason!

Well, guess what–I had a ticket to Paris. My name was

now Greg Johnson and I was assigned aisle seats on flights to Philadelphia and beyond. The younger guy with the beard in the passport photo looked about as much like clean-shaven me as he looked like a clean-shaven Scott. I would have to take the luggage I had found on this bed with me and ditch my own gym bag, wallet and ID until my return trip was over. Scott's–Greg's–tickets were one-way. But I could pay my own way home with Scott's dollars. Tomorrow–no it was already 1:20 a.m. today–was Monday, May 6 and I was due back at the *Record* on Saturday afternoon, the 12th. I had five days to sort it out.

The whole idea of flying to Paris, where I had never been, as Greg Johnson, someone I was not, excited and unnerved me at the same time. And being all alone in a motel room that wasn't mine didn't help; the jumpiness I felt came right through my anger at Scott and at Laura. Even after I put the photos away, I couldn't help seeing that snapshot of them together, as I tried to settle down to the ordinary details of travel.

To dress respectably for a transatlantic flight, I would have to ditch the worn and sporty stuff I'd packed for my weekend–wearing it would make other passengers notice me. Domestic flights were often getting somewhat casual now, but most people flying overseas wanted to look their best. I'd have to wear Scott's suits, but we were close to the same size and build. For the beach weekend I had brought only tennis shoes. I unwrapped one of Scott's black wingtips from the suitcase, size eleven-and-a-half. I wore elevens. Maybe I'd have to pull my athletic socks on first, and then Scott's black dress socks over them, but I could probably make that work.

The day had wrung me out, and if I was going to get any rest before the flight it had better start soon. I crept out to the Ford to get my own bag, locked the car and hung the

"Do Not Disturb" sign on the knob outside the room. Then I soaked my wrist in hot water in the basin and took a warm shower, shrugging the stress out of my neck and shoulders. The little framed card on the inside of the motel door said checkout time was 11 a.m., but Scott's flight was due to take off ten minutes before that, so I set the alarm clock beside the TV for 7:15 a.m., got into my own pajamas and into Gregory Johnson's motel bed and tried to sleep.

Fat chance! It was already 2:30 a.m. but my mind was a maze where thoughts kept colliding. The first thing I thought of was a danger sign I had ignored. Very early in our marriage, during the three months when I was in Germany and Laura was still in the States, she had had a flirtation with a guy we both had known in college. Another college chum of mine wrote to warn me about it. He didn't actually call it an affair, just hinted that it could be, but he wanted me to know. I stewed about it, but it was almost time for Laura to fly into Frankfurt and I was so happy to have her that when she arrived, I didn't want to spoil the moment by confronting her first thing. In the end, I forgave her without telling her and without ever knowing if there was really anything to forgive. If there was, I assumed she had been lonely for me and it was better forgotten.

Well, apparently, I'd had that wrong.

But, if I was always faithful, I wasn't always blameless either. For instance, she probably knew that I didn't see her career as an artist the same way she did. Laura had some talent, I thought, and perhaps the passion to support it, but not the discipline. She wasn't willing to work hard enough to make the splash she expected. I had helped her find the artist's cooperative where she rented space, but it was filled with half-finished paintings she had left to go on to something new. And while I couldn't blame her that she liked painting but was tired of hunting galleries or other places to exhibit her work, I could see that the art world was more competitive than she had thought. I wasn't holding my breath for a big breakthrough.

There were other problems too. Once Laura got the Pill, soon after we left college, she just assumed that took care of the question of having children, so there was our difference about that. But, when I thought about it, there was lots more. Laura and I had grown apart without ever talking about it. After midnight we slept in the same bed, but in the daylight, we probably hadn't faced each other honestly for a long time.

Sometimes, when I was home and she wasn't yet, I had imagined myself dating someone else as if I had never even met Laura. So, after I saw her wrecked VW in the surf, I began to think I might have wished my own wife out of existence. That's such a heavy thing to try to live with that eventually I had to set up a private appointment with Kathleen Metzer, the therapist who ran our group sessions. It was not easy, but I confessed that to her.

Kathleen was one smart lady. "Oh," she told me, "that's pretty common in survivors, but you have to understand it's magic thinking. It's no different than when a little girl is angry at her mother and tells her, 'I wish you were dead!' and then if for some reason the mother dies, the girl believes she has killed her. That can mess someone up with regrets they don't deserve for a long time."

Getting over that childish idea was the biggest help I had gotten from therapy, but tonight I saw that I had struggled with guilt when the real guilt had been Laura's all along. I had been blindsided by her death, but now I was blindsided and enraged at her deceit. And if she wanted out, why wouldn't a divorce have been enough? It takes a while in California, but she'd have been free to do whatever she wanted from the day she filed. I couldn't imagine that she really wanted to *kill* me. There was no reason for that.

Well, there was *someone* with a reason, of course–Scott. How arrogant he'd been! But Laura must have fallen for him so badly that she believed whatever he said. When he sat on our couch after our dinner, and entertained us with his stories, he'd been showing off for Laura, not for the two of us.

And tonight–how helpless I must have looked when he found me in his laundry room, doing domestic work and wearing his short pants! But that had probably been my good luck–he wasn't expecting a fight.

I wouldn't sleep as long as I thought about Scott, so I tried my best to understand Laura's part in it all. Still, empty and betrayed as I felt, I couldn't help remembering how she had looked at bedtime when we were newly married, sitting in front of our second-hand vanity, brushing her long blonde hair. But it was a memory that had turned bitter now.

A little before dawn, I think, I fell into a doze that didn't end till I heard the alarm at 7:15 and woke to a sore wrist, a light headache and a travel day I'd never planned.

17.

I shaved and dressed in Scott's dark blue pinstripe suit and his light blue button-down shirt, both of which fit well enough, and chose a blue and green rep tie. I downed two aspirin and put my own toiletries kit into the green briefcase-bag, then checked Scott's to make sure there was no identity card or address in it and slipped it into my gym bag to leave behind.

While I thought about destroying the photos of Laura I hesitated, then put them back into the bag that would go with me to Paris. If she didn't come to the airport, as I hoped, I might need to select one or two to show to anyone I could find to help me. But she would come, wouldn't she, for a romantic reunion with Scott after so much time apart?

Using two dollars from Greg Johnson's wallet, I left the motel cleaning lady a tip under the clock by the TV. I intended to pay for breakfast with those bills too. On this trip, I'd use Scott's cash from here on out; I could never spend as much as he owed me now.

It was just after eight when I drove away from the motel carrying two wallets–Greg Johnson's in my left inside suit pocket and my own in the right. I didn't want to give my own up yet. The flight to Philadelphia was scheduled for 10:50 a.m. That meant boarding would begin about 10:20, and I should be at the airport, some seven more miles up El Camino, by 9:30, so I drove to the same diner where I'd had coffee ten hours earlier–anything familiar seemed comforting now.

The morning papers on the racks outside, my own

Record-Courier and the *Chronicle,* both had nothing about a San Francisco dentist's murder in Monterey, and I would have been surprised if they had. Even the last editions' deadlines would have come too soon after the fire.

Inside, a different crew was on and a plump, motherly looking lady with a squint was behind the counter. She poured coffee for me as soon as I asked, while I looked the menu over. "I'm in kind of a hurry," I said. "Would it take long to make oatmeal?"

"No, honey. We use instant–we can whip it up any time."

"Fine, I'll have oatmeal and waffles and bacon." Because the menu offered 'Belgium Waffles' and the copy editor in me couldn't let it slide, I asked, "How do you make your Belgian waffles?"

"Same as everywhere," she said. "Just, oil, water and waffle mix."

I knew better than that. Ever since our trip to England, when we had driven our old Opel across Belgium to take the ferry, I had been a fan of Belgian Waffles. At breakfast in Ostend, a waitress had explained that it was yeast, and the dough rising overnight, that made them so light and crispy.

So now I asked, "Then what makes Belgian waffles better than plain waffles?"

"The waffle-iron. We use a Belgium waffle-iron–bigger holes to hold more syrup."

I correct copy, not people. "Makes sense," I said.

The coffee was still too weak–half the strength of newsroom coffee–but the food, when it came, was sturdy and good enough. The bacon was crisp. My headache was gone. Oddly, my mood was better than I had a right to expect. Driving back from Monterey the night before, I had been shaken to think that I had killed a man, even if he was aiming a gun at me. This morning I knew more of the truth and felt justified for everything–resolute and level-headed for the first time since the escape from Monterey. My left wrist was still tender, but only slightly swollen and I couldn't complain. After all, I was alive.

Back in the car, I switched the Motorola on, but the station that called itself "all-news" had nothing. Local radio and TV usually followed the press–their small staffs used newspapers as tip sheets, and sometimes just rewrote what the papers had.

On the way to San Francisco International, I pulled into a Shell station in Burlingame for gas, because the gauge showed a quarter-tank and I might want a full one when I got back. While a husky young attendant checked the oil and tires and wiped the windshield, I had my last chance to decide–was I really going to do this?

Yes. I'd set out once to be a reporter, and my high school journalism teacher had taught us the first day that anyone could do it in two simple steps: first find out, then make the report. If you got the truth–all of it you needed–there was nothing tough about step two–putting your report on paper.

"Sure, the art that goes into writing makes it better," she said, "but even without it you *are* a reporter."

So if my wife was still alive, I'd never know what the story was until I did the legwork–until I found out. And if she was hiding out in Paris, I wanted to see her again, if only to let her know that I knew it, and that I was still alive but her lover most definitely was not. I drove away from the station with my path clear, and not just because the windshield had been polished.

At the airport I parked in the long-term lot–who knew how long the term would be? Taking my own billfold, with my Social Security card and driver's license and the dollars I had left, I sank it under the jumble of clothes and tennis shoes in my own little weekend bag. Then, since the station wagon had no trunk, I hurriedly put that bag down on the floor in front of the passenger seat and covered it with an old raincoat I kept in the Ford for bad weather. Now I was Gregory Johnson.

There was not a thing but clothing that had once belonged to Scott in Greg Johnson's suitcase, but, aside from his billfold in my pocket, everything I needed to keep with me, from my underwear to plane tickets to envelopes of cash–was in his fabric briefcase. Now it had become my carry-on, and it would have to stay with me, so when the shuttle bus to the terminal pulled up, and the driver took it from me and shoved it onto a rack with Johnson's suitcase and the other passengers' luggage, I picked a seat across the aisle to keep it in view.

I walked up to the short line at the AA ticket desk as deliberately as I could but feeling queasy about presenting my false passport. The red-haired young fellow who took it did study the photo and look up at my face for a moment, but then he smiled and nodded as if to say, *Oh, I see. You've matured a bit and shaved.* I relaxed. As he checked my suitcase through to Paris and directed me to Gate A7, he spoke with a bit of an Irish burr, and I felt international already.

The concourse was uncrowded as I ambled out to gate A7. It was a relief to be rid of the suitcase–I could switch the carry-on to my right hand and rest my tender left wrist. A display above the boarding desk at gate A4 announced a flight to Mexico City that was about to load and in the A4 waiting area there was standing room only. Family members were saying good-by to each other with embraces, so there were probably more well-wishers than travelers. Passengers at my gate had longer to wait for boarding, and the crowd I found there was smaller.

I had to show Scott's fake ID, once more, to the slightly

chubby young woman at the A7 counter, and I was uneasy again, but I could have saved my angst; she gave it a glance, handed the pass back to me, smiled the required smile, and told me what I already knew: "22C, Left side."

I was happy to be sitting with the rabble–Scott might have afforded First Class, but the slim chance that a wealthier passenger there would recognize him from his social life or dental practice probably was the last chance he had wanted to take. That was fine with me. I wanted to go unnoticed too.

There were twenty-five minutes till boarding. The 707 was already at the gate, so I went to the terminal's big windows for a look. It was larger than any airliner I had been on. The moveable boarding gangway obscured one side, but from a second terminal window I could see the nose and one silver wing with two big jet engines.

In August 1963, when Laura and I had come back from Germany with a planeload of returning GI's and their wives, we had been on a chartered Lockheed Constellation, a four-engine prop plane that made the trip in three hops, to Shannon Airport in Ireland, where we had all gotten off to have supper in a dining room set aside for us, then Gander, Newfoundland, where we had all eaten breakfast, then Idlewild in New York by afternoon. That had taken us about twenty-six hours in all.

It was a heady idea that, even flying against, and not with, the sun, two jetliners could get me from San Francisco to Paris before noon tomorrow.

Twenty minutes to wait. I visited the men's room, and then, realizing that the first street edition of what was now the lone afternoon paper, the *Examiner*, might be out, I went back down the concourse to the newsstand I'd passed.

There it was, across the top of Page One:

S.F. SOCIALITE SLAIN;
BEACH HOUSE BURNS

So editors at the *Ex* had decided to promote Scott from 'society dentist' to 'socialite.' I guessed the *Record* would do the same tomorrow morning.

18.

I bought the *Ex* and went back to the waiting passengers at Gate A7, dropped into a seat and read the story. It began:

> A battered body, believed to be that of Scott Croswell, prominent San Francisco philanthropist and man-about-town, was recovered from the charred remains of his luxurious vacation home on Monterey Bay today, after the house was leveled in an overnight fire.
>
> Authorities called the fire "arson," the death "murder."
>
> "And it's one of the most brutal murders I've ever had to investigate," said Detective Sgt. Walter Talcott of the Monterey Police. "When he was cornered, Dr. Croswell appears to have fought back fiercely."
>
> Croswell, a dentist who served many society leaders, was known to vary his weekends often between casinos at Lake Tahoe and his secluded Monterey bachelor pad.
>
> Broken bones testified that Croswell had been savagely beaten before the killer or killers spread gasoline to torch the house and the body....

The story was by Carl Silver, a byline I didn't know.

Though I scanned the *Examiner* every afternoon at work, I rarely had time to read it closely. It was a good, workman-like job I thought, but as an editor I couldn't help looking at it critically. Of course, it was wrong about Scott being cornered and "fighting back" but that was what the police believed. Promoting Scott to "philanthropist" was a stretch, but one the *Ex* might excuse. "Luxurious home" was probably okay, it would seem luxurious to most readers, and "bachelor pad" was right on. I admired the second sentence: "Authorities called the fire "arson," the death "murder." That had impact.

The detective's quote that followed was a good one, but with a problem. It read beautifully out of that short line because it began with "And," but I doubted that the cop had ever said that word. If he was answering a reporter's question, he wouldn't have begun with "And." At my paper, unless we were really against the deadline, I would have left the copy desk to ask the reporter about that. You don't want to make up quotes even by one word. Soon, you might be tempted to make up whole quotes—a firing offense at responsible papers.

There was a sign of enterprise in the next paragraph, however—news, even to me. Carl Silver had reached someone, one of Scott's dental assistants or society patients perhaps, who knew he often went to the Tahoe casinos across the Nevada state line. That was something I'd never heard him mention—in fact, he had concealed that pretty well. It made my hunch about financial woes more likely. Scanning the rest of the story quickly, I also learned that "fire crews struggled to save a threatened stand of eucalyptus trees next to the house." I hadn't considered that the trees were in danger, but if firemen did need to put hoses on them, that might have slowed putting out the blaze at the house itself.

The boarding announcement came just then, and I joined the line, gave up my pass to the young lady who'd checked it earlier, and shuffled onto the big plane. It was a long way back to row 22 but my seat was still a little in front of the tips of the new swept-back wings. I put Greg Johnson's green carry-on bag at my feet under the seat in front of me for safety, nodded to the balding guy at the window seat who was reading a business book, went back to the *Examiner's* story, and hoped that the middle seat would stay unoccupied.

It did until the last minute. Then a boy 15 or 16 years old came down the aisle in a hurry and plopped his own stuffed bag under it. He arrived dressed in slacks, tie, tan sport coat, and horn rim glasses like any traveling man, but looking like a very young and anxious one.

"Well, you just made it," I told him. "Bad traffic?"

"Naw, I'm coming from Boise and I was supposed to get in three hours ago, but my plane never even took off. They had to put me on two different ones. I just got here, through Reno. My names Thomas Stafford, what's yours?"

"Greg Johnson," I said without hesitating. "What do you like to be called, Thomas or Tommy?"

"My Grandparents call me Thomas and my folks call me Tommy, but my friends call me Tom." He was a good-looking kid, the kind they would use in TV ads–open-faced, dark-haired, and tanned.

"So you're going to Philadelphia by yourself, Tom?"

"Naw–all the way to Germany, well, Philadelphia first. Sixteen of us are going to meet there and have four days of orientation before we fly to Frankfurt next Saturday. I'm in Global Understanding–the, uh, student exchange program. How long do you think it will be till they give us lunch?"

"Hard to say–two-three hours maybe."

"Okay, then…." He frowned. "Shoot!"

"Did you miss a meal?"

"Yeah. I was supposed to have breakfast on that plane that didn't go. 'Haven't had anything since last night."

The 707 had not yet pushed back, and a pretty stewardess in a dark blue uniform and cap had just finished helping a lady in the seats ahead get her cosmetics case into the overhead bins. I stood up. "Pardon me. I wonder if you could help my friend, Tom, here? He's traveling alone all the way to Germany, and he missed breakfast. Is there any way he could get some food before lunch?"

She leaned in toward the middle seat, "Hi, Tommy. I'm Annie. I'm afraid we can't do a lunch early, but I can get you some snacks and a drink to tide you over. Would you rather have a Coke, apple juice or milk?"

"Milk, I guess." The girl winked at him and left.

"Good choice," I said. "Milk's better at breakfast."

"I had two Cokes yesterday–I'm really going to miss them in Germany!"

"No, I don't think so. The first town square I saw in Germany had big round red signs advertising Coke."

"You were in Germany!

"In the Army–draftee–six years ago now, and nearly twenty after the big war there," I said. "And Germany had Cokes everywhere I'm afraid."

"Really?"

"Yep. You know, those signs even looked exactly like the ones at home–big red buttons that say 'Drink Coca-Cola, Refresh,' only these said, '*Trink* Coca-Cola *Eiskalt*' so I thought I'd learned two new German words."

"Drink and refresh?"

"Yep. But I was half right. As a matter of fact, *Eiskalt* means Ice cold!"

"Oh!"

"Right after that I ordered my first lunch in a German

restaurant–that's tricky, but it went okay. So afterward, when the waitress asked me, 'Vas good, yes?' I showed off by saying, *'Ja! Ich bin Eiskalt!'*"

"Oh, oh."

"Yeah, oh, oh. She gave me a really funny look. But it wasn't till I first told that story to a German family that they burst out laughing. By then I'd learned that Germans don't say 'I'm cold'–they say *'Es ist mir kalt'* or 'It's cold to me.' But what I didn't know is that, in German, if you say what I said to the waitress, you're saying that you just aren't good at lovemaking, if you get the idea."

Tom was quick. He snickered and put one hand over his mouth. "*Frigid!*" he whispered too loudly.

"Exactly!"

But after my evening with Misty, the story had an uncomfortable edge I hadn't anticipated.

"I hope I don't say something like that!" Tom said.

"You probably will, so get over it now. The Germans really seem to enjoy it."

When she went down the aisle checking seat belts, Annie slipped Tom a Milky Way, a Hershey bar and two packs of peanuts. "Milk as soon as we're airborne," she said quietly and moved on. Tom gave her a dazzling smile. In search of global understanding, I thought, he and some German girl were likely to break each other's hearts in the year ahead.

Tom turned to me and started on the Milky Way. "Thanks!" he said. "Did you like Germany?"

"Sure! Winters can be a little grim, but not at Christmas or Fasching. Fasching is like Mardi Gras, but better, and it goes on longer. Summers are terrific. You're going to get there at a good time."

Lunch when it came was chicken Kiev, and really pretty good. In '68, because government set all the fares, the airlines were still using their menus to compete for passengers, even advertising the names of famous chefs that they claimed dreamed them up. So my new friend, Tom Stafford, and I ate happily and talked about Germany most of the way to Philly—reassuring for him, I think, and a break I needed from my own thoughts.

About an hour out of Philadelphia, I went back five or six rows to the lavatory, and when I came out, the pretty stew who'd told Tom she was Annie was leaning against the counter in the galley, taking a break and sipping cola from a plastic glass. She had taken her uniform cap off for a moment and her soft brown hair swung when she turned my way. Her blue uniform set off her bright blue eyes. "Hey, Annie," I said. "That was kind of you. Thanks!"

"Kind of you, too," she said. "Kids traveling alone are usually too shy to say what they need."

"Does American always carry candy bars aboard?"

She gave me a mischievous smile. "It does when I fly—I always have at least two in my purse. Just like Tommy, I've sometimes missed meals."

"Really?"

"Pilots eat first, passengers next, flight crews last, and sometimes—not often—we're short a meal or two.

"So you gave him your own? Now I *am* impressed. I guess I owe you some candy bars—or maybe a box. Can you tell me where to send it?"

Annie was amused. "You know we can't give out addresses to passengers!" She pretended to pout at my misstep, but the way she looked at me out of the corners of her eyes raised my hopes.

"Well, then I might at least want to write to the airline about your helpfulness. Tell me your last name anyway, and where you're based—that's not an address."

She smiled, looked down at her drink glass, as if

considering. "It's Anderson, and Annie is just an airline nickname. Really, it's Inger, so you can see why I don't use it. And San Francisco is home base, but I don't live there; most of us live in Burlingame, close to the airport. She suddenly looked away and lifted her chin as if to dismiss me. "Now, no more questions."

I gave her a smile and a half-wave and went back to my seat. I worked for a newspaper. If I ever wanted to look her up, I had enough.

Let's see, "Annie Anderson, real name: Inger; Stewardess, American Airlines. Based at S.F.O. but lives (rents) in Burlingame, probably with other stews. About 5'8" tall; age prob. 26 to 29; blue-eyed brunette (large eyes, bow mouth, nice legs.) Likes: travel, kids, candy. Aspect: attentive, kind, cute, no nonsense."

Yes, I had enough to find her, and to convince me I might want to someday.

19.

Philly was still light when we landed at around 6:30, local time. I had only 50 minutes between planes and wanted to grab an airport snack, so I yanked my carry-on out from under the seat as soon as the seat belt light went out and got into the line forming in the aisle. Tom was right behind me, eager to meet fellow exchange students or his welcoming party.

I would have liked to trade addresses with him, but that wouldn't work either way. I'd told him I was Greg Johnson and giving him my real address might tie it to my false ID, And if I mailed to his address, I'd have a hard time trying to explain why I'd given him a phony name.

As we worked our way along the aisle, ducking small bags being lifted out of the overhead bins, I said, "Well, it was nice to meet you, Tom. Have a good year in Germany."

"Nice to meet you too, Mr. Johnson. I probably learned more about Germany from you than I will in orientation."

"Remember, mine's old info. For all I know, Germany banned Coca-Cola last year."

When we neared the waiting room, I let him pass me in the boarding tunnel, then saw him head directly to a smiling middle-aged couple holding a "Thomas Stafford" sign. He grinned and waved at me as the three of them left together.

* * *

It was growing dark enough that Philadelphia was beginning to light up when we flew out at about 7:30. Surprisingly, this plane was only two-thirds full, and since

Scott had gotten seat 24C, fairly far back in the smoking section, I had seats A, B and C to myself and a chance to sleep. Maybe Scott had hoped for that for himself, or at least to avoid having an inquisitive person, like Tom, next to him.

One of the good things about travel, I thought, was chance encounters with interesting people that you'd never see again. Tom was well-spoken, personable, smart and really inquisitive–he had the stuff to become a fine reporter, and some day he might do exactly that–but if he did, I'd never know it. So many people come and go in your life with no lasting significance.

Actually, in Tom's case, I had that last thought wrong, but I didn't learn until much later how great his significance in my life had been. After all, just by being hungry, he had more or less introduced me to Annie.

* * *

Not long after we reached cruising altitude, the distant lights of a big city–Boston, I guessed–went by on our left and then we were flying over black water. I settled back in my seat to rest and realized immediately how tired I was. I'd hardly slept the two nights before, and the days had been emotional and exhausting. Another stewardess was coming up the aisle offering small pillows. I took one and asked, "Is it okay if I just put up the armrests and sleep across all three seats?"

"That's what I'd do if I was lucky enough to get three seats together."

"I'm surprised there are so many empty, isn't tourist season starting?"

"Well, we're flying lighter tonight. I think some people delayed travel because of the Paris riots. They were pretty bad today, I guess." She moved on briskly to the row behind me.

At the *Record* on Friday night, my last shift before my week off, I had compiled an AP dispatch and one from UPI to make a more complete story about a big student uprising in Paris. AP had the best lead, but UPI had better student quotes. That story had been on street racks and doorsteps Saturday while I was driving the Porsche to Monterey. I'd lost track of the uprising for a couple of days, but apparently it was still going on. I hadn't counted on that. It could make Laura harder to find.

'Nothing I could do about it now. I lifted the armrests and curled up across the three seats, hoping to sleep through a very short night, but for another hour or so, tired as I was, no sleep came. It was good to have three seats to myself, but it had been better to have Tom sitting next to me. Talking to him about Germany had blotted out all the tension and sorrow of the last two days. Now, by myself, I had time to think again about how devastating it was to lose your "best friend" and your "beloved wife" all at once.

How could Laura, so casual and chatty on a weekday morning, be hoping to be all alone with Scott once I'd left for work in the afternoon? How could Scott, in that little café on Mason Street, listen so sympathetically over his pancakes to my sorrow about my wife's death and still be scheming to do me in?

With a pang, I saw suddenly that they were not the only ones I had lost. Now Misty, was gone too. In that big chair on Saturday night, I'd had the fleeting thought that, though I had known her for less than a day, I *might* even love Misty. But now that she was dead, I knew that, in one way at least, that was true, just because I *cared* so much about her death. Losing her young life had been unfair, unnecessary, unjustifiable–a pointless loss, and a personal loss to me. She'd been a bright spot in my life–hopeful and playful in spite of being robbed hours before we met. And, unlike Scott or Laura, she had been honest with me about her feelings. She was a tease and an opportunist, but she had a conscience of some sort–something Scott and Laura could have used.

It came to me then that if I had *known* I loved Misty, I probably could have shown her that I did. Maybe that was the answer I'd been looking for on Saturday night as I sat alone on the beach.

Sometime after that, I slept.

20.

When I woke Tuesday, we had already flown into dawn, but we were still somewhere over the water. I set my watch ahead to Paris time, 9:15 a.m., and soon after the cabin crew delivered a continental breakfast. Once that was gone, I put my tray table back up, and moved over to the window to discover that we were now flying over tiny fields and villages.

Around 10:30, another stewardess–pleasant enough but businesslike and without Annie's sparkle–came around to offer a second cup of coffee, and the sound of the engines dropped lower as the plane began its long descent. A little later, just after I'd handed the empty cup back, I got my first glimpse of Paris. The city was huge, and unlike any other I'd seen from the air, even in Germany. Far out on the western outskirts we flew past a cluster of some modest skyscrapers, but in town the buildings all seemed to be a uniform height–about six or seven stories–and it was the monuments that dominated things. To the north of us I could identify the massive Arch of Triumph, because all the boulevards, lined with trees and crowded with little cars, seemed to radiate away from it like rays from the sun. Nearer to the plane, the Eiffel Tower stood, taller than anything else in the city, with the river curving before it and a great green lawn behind. But then we banked to the right and suddenly I was looking only at the 707's wing and the sky, and when we leveled off Paris was everywhere again but the landmarks I knew from photos and the old black-and-white newsreels of my childhood were gone.

As we settled into a landing pattern for Paris-Orly, I began to feel uneasy. Maybe there would be no one waiting at the gate and no sure way to know where Laura could be, if she was even in Paris. I had only a couple of days and, with civic chaos in the way, I might be in for a fruitless search of art schools and studios in a place where I didn't speak the language. People always called Paris charming, but no one mentioned that it was gigantic, and now I'd seen for myself that it certainly wasn't compact like San Francisco. Laura would be expecting Scott, more than likely, but would she meet him eagerly at the airport or be waiting somewhere for him to come to her? Then too, if she spotted me before I saw her would she vanish? I'd have to pay close attention from the moment I left the plane. My anger at her when I'd found those photos had made me too impulsive; I'd been foolish about finding her easily.

When the 707 jolted onto the runway, headed for the terminal and rolled past a long line of planes to its arrival gate, I tried to get my bearings. There was nothing Old World about the Orly terminal. It was all steel columns and glass walls. We finally came to a stop and sat for a minute or two, then a chime sounded, and seat belts clicked as passengers scrambled to pull luggage out of the overhead bins. I hung back a bit, with Scott's carry-on bag at my feet. I was anxious, but not anxious to be among the first off. Eventually there were only about a dozen people behind me, and I took my place in line.

In flight we'd all been given a landing card for customs and we'd filled them out to save time–I had nothing to declare–but instead of going to a waiting room as I expected, we were herded down a flight of stairs into a large, windowless arrival hall.

Suddenly, my stomach felt empty; in America my false passport hadn't caused a ripple, but in a foreign country it might. I joined one of the lines that led to officials in uniform who seemed to be taking an interest in every detail. Occasionally, they were picking out passengers and sending them to a row of tables for further processing.

But I was lucky. The bored, white-haired official who glanced at my landing card and collected it seemed only interested in verifying that my passport was from the U.S.A. and didn't pause at its phony photo.

Safely away from the inspection station, I toted my little green bag up a crowded escalator and through an exit door, and suddenly found myself in a very busy but wide-open baggage area, with a long wall of glass that gave a view of the cars and taxis on the street outside. I felt exposed; Laura could be anywhere. There was a fixed row of stylish steel-and-leather airport seating beside me, and a newspaper someone had abandoned, *Le Figaro*, rested in one seat. I snatched it up as if to hide my nakedness and opened it in front of me like an intent reader as I settled into the seat.

A long moving belt was delivering luggage to stations along the terminal wall opposite the windows, and porters were lifting it off. Peering over the paper, I picked out several passengers I recognized from our plane at one station, so that's where our suitcases would arrive, and if Laura were to show up, where the arrivals board would send her. I moved to another row of seats, closer, but not directly across from that station. There was no sign of Laura–a bad omen. She was seldom late, and she should have been early for Scott. Over the next twenty minutes as I sat there, I watched dismayed as luggage arrived and more and more people from my plane picked up theirs and vanished, until there were only five or six suitcases left standing by the moving belt–one of them Scott's. I'd wait to claim it until the porters started to take it away, but I felt defeated. My hunch hadn't paid off and I couldn't decide what to do next.

Still peering over *Le Figaro*, I turned one more time to look down the long, crowded corridor of steel columns and glass. Far away, a blonde in a light green dress was weaving in and out of the bunches of pedestrians like a broken-field runner, hurrying this way. My stomach jumped. Her hair was cut shorter, but it was Laura–I'd know her anywhere the way her hips swung; I'd once kidded her that she had taken walking lessons from Marilyn Monroe. I sat waiting behind my paper, feeling apprehensive, keyed up, and ready to pounce. She went directly to Scott's leather suitcase as if she knew it well, then looked around frantically for her lover. Wearing Scott's suit, I rose and started toward her before I dropped the paper away from my eyes. A radiant smile crossed her face, then twisted in an instant as she went pale and slid down quickly to sit on Scott's leather suitcase. Her silky skirt settled over it like a dejected afterthought.

21.

Just for a moment, I felt sorry for her. This wasn't going to be as satisfying as I'd imagined.

"Hello, Laura," I said quietly. Let's move to the chairs over there. I'll help you. Scott couldn't make it, so I came instead." I gave her my arm and she leaned on it as if her legs were weak and her loving husband was supporting her. We crossed the 20 feet to the nearest row of seats wordlessly and both sat down.

"I thought you'd get here earlier," I said, to delay the rest.

Her eyes slid fearfully, avoiding mine. "Paris is a mess!" she said. "The students are rioting, and police are mauling them, and traffic is jammed up wherever you try to go–but it's all there in your paper!" she said, pointing at *Le Figaro*. I had been looking over it, not at it, but the type was black across the top of Page One and a deep two-column photo showed an angry young man hurling a stone while flames billowed from windows behind him. I'd seen similar shots in papers and on TV at home lately, but with fires in strip malls, not stone buildings.

"Where's Scott?" Laura demanded suddenly.

"He's in Monterey."

"Is he in jail?"

"No, Laura, he's dead."

Her jaw hardened and her eyes narrowed as if she were recalculating the rest of her life. "I told him it wouldn't work," she said. "Can we get out of here?"

"Of course. Do you have a car somewhere?"

115

"In the garage across the way."

"Then let's go. Can you walk okay?"

"Certainly!" she said as if I'd insulted her, as if I hadn't just had to help her to a chair. She stood up immediately and headed for the exit. I grabbed the carry-on, left the suitcase where it stood, and caught up with her. Outside, we crossed with a group while a guard held up the heavy traffic, took a crowded elevator to the roof level and had a long, brisk walk to a black Mercedes sedan, all without a word.

"Nice car." I said.

"I rented it yesterday–for a reunion," she said bitterly.

"Can you give me the keys? I'm going to drive."

She handed them over, no complaint. "Just don't head into Paris. They're building barricades and prying cobblestones out of the street to throw!"

"We'll go south." While our plane was circling before landing, I had seen two towns to the south, one at each corner of the airport, and what looked like green woods in the far distance.

The Mercedes was a challenge–several feet longer and maybe twice as heavy as the Porsche had been, with a hood long enough to shorten my view of the road, so I couldn't pretend to drive casually. We threaded our way out through the airport traffic first to the east and then south, through the crooked streets of one of the towns–the sign said *Villeneuve-le-Roi*. With no real plan, and no idea what would come next, I said nothing, trying not to show how shaky I felt. Laura sat stiffly beside me, holding back anger and whatever shock she was feeling about Scott's death. I could sometimes hear her silence broken by a sharp intake of breath. But when we were out of the town, she suddenly turned toward me and said, "Look! Just tell me this: Did Scott tell you how to find me?"

"No, Laura. He told me two things–that I was a moron, and that I messed things up. His gun told me the rest."

"Then how did you know where I was?"

"Just followed the clues."

My answers exasperated her. "Well! Aren't *you* the hard-boiled detective!"

"Soft-boiled, maybe."

"*Soft-boiled is right!* Always so damn self-effacing! Always so *nice.*"

I let it drop. Arguments could wait. I was tense enough just driving an unfamiliar car on a foreign two-lane road.

I thought about it for a minute though: I wasn't much of a detective. I hadn't really uncovered any clues, just come across them like someone on a treasure hunt–the gas can, the room key, the ticket to Paris, and I'd been sent impulsively wherever they suggested, without really asking what came next. Now I was in Paris–next to it, anyway–and in over my head. I had no idea where we were and no plan but to hope it turned out okay.

After a few more miles, fields gave way to woods on both sides of the highway and I finally saw a chance for some privacy, a place to turn off to the right on a gravel road into the trees, I crept along it for about 200 yards until there was another side road to the left, then a chance to turn right again until the road became just a track in the spring-green woods.

When the oaks and silver maples were closer together and the track was growing uneven, the Mercedes began to rock on its springs. I stopped in the shade, cut the engine, cranked the window down and listened–rustle of leaves, distant drone of an airliner, no voices. I rolled up the window again and turned to look at Laura. "Well?"

"Well, what?"

I think you have some things to tell me."

She gave me a steely look. "You *murdered* Scott!

"He's dead. It wasn't murder. And I'm not sorry!"

Rage twisted her face– I thought she might hit me.

"How could you do it? I wouldn't have thought you could!"

It was my turn to be infuriated. "How could I do it? I'll tell you how–self-defense! He had a gun on me–four feet away. He'd shot and killed a girl he didn't even know–in her sleep! I smashed out the light and the room went black. He shot at me anyway–twice! And trying to knock the gun away I beat him to death! I beat him to death! That's how I could do it, Laura–I beat him to death in the dark with a hot steam iron!" I was breathing hard just from the anger and the telling.

Laura turned away from me, doubled over, and covered her face. She was moaning, keening, but softly, like a hurt creature trying not to let predators know her hiding place.

"I didn't intend to kill him, but he had the gun. And I'm not sorry."

"He killed a girl?"

I calmed down and told her pretty much the whole story, and finished by saying, "I went out down the beach for a while that night, and in the morning, I found her with a bullet in her head. I guess Scott was too chicken to kill me in person. He shot right through the blanket. You've both got that on your conscience now."

"Scott doesn't. He's gone."

"But you do?"

"Yes."

There were tears in her eyes now, but not on her face, and her jaw was set hard. The car went quiet.

I leaned back against the driver's seat and waited.

It was a fine day in France. There was a soft blue afternoon sky where I could see it between the treetops ahead of us. Little white clouds followed each other, one by one, in a slow parade across that space–smaller than California clouds. Thinking of the chaos and hurt in Paris, and of the two of us alone, and wary, in this car in the woods, I wondered how often life's miseries arrived on its sunniest days.

Then again, I said, "Well?"

"What?"

"I know you and Scott were having an affair and tried to kill me. And, I've seen the photos of you that Scott took–Polaroids too–they were in his carry-on."

That shook her; she cowered and bit her lip.

"Now tell me the rest. You owe me that. We're going to stay here till I hear it."

"I don't have to tell you anything. Ever!

I switched from bad cop to good cop. "Look, Laura, I know you're hurting now. I've been grieving for *you* for four months. Think of how it was for me just two or three weeks out–Valentine's Day. So I know how it feels. But we're really in this together now. I hid the girl's body. I put her in the ocean. That makes me an accomplice to murder. When Scott killed her it was a mistake, but it's still murder because he meant to kill me. You had to know all about his plan, so you're an accomplice too–we both are. But the cops have no clue. They don't know about the girl and they never saw me. They probably think Scott owed somebody or crossed somebody and it was just revenge or something. So you might as well tell me all of it."

It was quiet again. In the woods off to the left, a mother quail and a line of five babies strutted through the dappled sunlight. Laura sat motionless beside me, considering, her head down and her hands on her knees, then suddenly turned toward me.

"It went so wrong! We didn't have any choice. We were

desperate–they were going to kill Scott and they threatened me too!" Her eyes were panicky, her lips an anxious grimace. She began to wring her hands in her lap.

"Threatened you? "Who?"

"Casino guys, collectors, goons, thugs, the mob! Who knows? Scott owed big money. His family in New York had it, and he liked baccarat. He'd inherited from his dad, so for years he'd played, and he mostly won–won lots more than he lost. Almost every weekend when he didn't go to Monterey. he drove up to Stateline and Tahoe. But then things flipped–he lost and lost. He'd pledged big donations at charity things in the city, but he put them off. At work, he managed to pay his staff, but he was way behind on their tax withholding. He said even the IRS would have it in for him."

"Okay," I said. "Start over. When did you and Scott first get together?"

She frowned. "I don't think you want to hear about that."

"Laura, I want to hear everything."

But she was right; I didn't a bit like hearing what came next: Their affair had started long before I imagined, more than a year ago and fairly soon after they met. Scott threw a pre-Christmas party at his apartment for his five-person staff and fifteen or twenty favored clients and friends. I was invited, but of course, I had to work that night until the last street edition, so Laura went alone. She stayed when the others left and the two of them got tipsy–or maybe it was stoned–and that's all I wanted to know about that.

22.

I studied my wife for a moment. The strain of confessing made her look older and worn and I was sorry. Maybe, somehow, I still cared about her but knowing what I knew meant everything was over and now I had to go on tormenting us both to get at the truth.

"So, how often did you see each other from then on?

"I told you, you don't want to hear it."

"I don't want to, but I have to!"

She looked down at her lap, not at me. Now, I thought, she seemed more ashamed than angry. The answer, when we got past all her evasiveness, was that they had been together at least once nearly every week. At the *Record*, Wednesdays were always overtime days. When we weren't editing the Thursday morning paper, we put together most of the back sections of the big Sunday edition for an early press run. Earlier, Laura had joined an artist co-op that rented a studio, and she'd often painted there, sometimes till midnight, on Wednesdays. But now in the evening she was there less and less, and with Scott more and more. Wednesday nights, I remembered, she'd sometimes come home smelling slightly of painter's turpentine, and that's a scent that can cancel out others, even booze and perfume. Some weekends, she went down to Carmel—right next to Monterey—to try to sell to the galleries, or so she'd told me. And because I had stayed in the Army Reserve for the extra pay after my discharge, the *Record* was required to give me two weeks off in July to swelter in Reserve Camp

121

at Fort Roberts—enough time for two long, cool casino weekends at Tahoe for the charming couple.

The more I wormed the truth out of her the angrier I felt. "So at some point you just thought it would be easier to shoot your husband rather than ask for a divorce?"

"Don't be mean."

"Oh—sorry! Thinking about a bullet through my head kind of brings that out in me. A slaying is so much kinder than an ugly divorce, don't you think?

"But it wasn't anything like that!" She was looking straight at me now, her eyes pleading for me to believe her.

"Scott wanted me to ask for a divorce, but I wasn't sure. He was on a losing streak, and he was being hounded by people he owed. He said I might even be in danger because of him, and for my safety, if we could fake my death, he'd send me here to Paris to do what I had always wanted to do, work with serious painters. He said he'd join me soon, either start winning again or just skip out on everyone he owed."

"That makes no sense. What would you live on?"

"Exactly what I said to him."

"So?"

"He said he didn't want to scare me, but he could still borrow on his business to send me here, and I'd be in danger if I didn't get out right away. I only gave in after he told me about the guy in the casino parking lot at Tahoe. It didn't—"

"Who was that?"

"I don't know! Just some guy—well-dressed big guy. Scott was in deep by then and this guy was waiting by his Porsche with a big picture the showroom photographer had taken of us together at dinner two weeks earlier. He showed it to Scott—they sold those, you know—souvenirs of your good time! Scott thought the guy wanted him to buy it. But he just handed it to Scott and said. 'That's a real pretty lady you've got, friend. It would be a crying shame if anything happened to her,' and he walked away!" Laura shivered. "Scott showed me the photo of us the guy gave him. So the plan was for my safety. That's when I agreed—last January."

"Where were you when this photo thing happened, up in Stateline?"

"Home in San Francisco that time."

"Scott told you this? And you believed it?"

"Yes!" Her brow furrowed as if she'd never considered anything else.

"But none of this really explains what just happened at the beach house, does it?

"No." She rubbed her forehead with the heel of her hand, as if to brush away something unpleasant.

"So that's what I need to know. Tell me."

"You're already too angry—it will only make you madder."

"Fine! Tell me."

Laura sighed. "Scott had to fly here last month to say what he needed to do by then. We were in debt—deep—he needed to act. Earlier he'd gotten the idea to change the beneficiaries on his life insurance policies to someone else and get himself fake ID to match. He did that after he'd lost too much, and he got fakes for me too, from an old ex-con, an engraver. When he was still in dental school, Scott had worked on the guy's teeth. So, the ID cost him some more, but now he could collect on his own insurance, if things got worse."

"I don't see how."

"Well, years back when he was flush—really winning thousands and thousands—he got two big life insurance policies. He made his sister's kids the beneficiaries but he didn't tell anyone. His family had done well by him, and he wanted to pay something back. If anything happened to him, he hoped his two nephews would both go to Cornell, like he had before dental school. But now he might need that money himself, and he fixed it so he could collect it instead."

"But he'd have to be dead for anyone to collect!"

"Well, he'd have to fake his death."

"So he'd need a body?"

She hung her head. "Yes."

"*My* body."

"Yes!"

I had seen that answer coming. Still, I felt like I'd been slapped.

23.

I glared at her. "How convenient! I'd be out of your way, Scott would get money, the goons would quit trying to collect–hey, how proud you two must have been of this brilliant plan!" She was frightened of me now–I could see it in her eyes.

"It was nothing like that. *We* didn't dream it up–Scott did–and that part came much later when there wasn't any other way out he could see. I never liked it! He took four days off and flew here last month to convince me. We couldn't really talk about it on the phone.

"Boy, this was the dumbest scheme I ever heard. For one thing, I'd be missing–due at work the next day or two. And 'his' corpse would have '*my*' fingerprints!"

No–I immediately saw that was wrong. Of course there would be no fingerprints after the housefire that the "collection men" would start.

And they had an answer for my sudden disappearance too. I'd said the right thing when I called their plan dumb–now Laura apparently had to defend it as clever. She admitted that after Scott did me in and torched his own house–with his leased Porsche in the garage–he was going to get back in my station wagon and drive all the way back to San Francisco and the big parking lot at the south end of the Golden Gate Bridge–that was what the vague note in the glove compartment was for, to make me look like a suicide jumper. After midnight that parking lot would be just about empty, and then he'd take the bike–stolen from a rack outside a school that same day–out of my car and pedal a mile or so through the quiet of the Presidio and then out a few blocks to the motels on Lombard Street. He planned to ditch the bike somewhere, hail a taxi or use a pay phone to call one, and then ride clear through town and out to the motel near the airport, where he would already have left his suitcase and papers when he drove down to Monterey for my murder.

"God, what a lot of trouble," I said. "All for a little insurance money."

"No! To save our lives! And for a new start together in Paris with new names and no debts. And it's not a little money, I don't call seven hundred thousand dollars little!"

That stopped me. I'd glanced at the insurance papers, but I hadn't looked inside to check the benefits. I was still trying to understand the ticket to Paris then, and after I'd found the photos of Laura and Scott I'd never gone back to the policies.

Now I took a minute to consider that $700,00 payoff. My pay was not bad for a newspaperman at that time–I made a decent living–but for what I was earning at the moment, even with raises, it might take something like 30 years to earn $700,000.

"Okay, so big money," I said. "But do you suppose insurance companies would pay that much out without using their own investigators? Sure, it would be his house that burned, but they'd want real ID for a burned-up body." I shook my head in disgust, "Dumb, Laura, dumb!"

"But they'd have the police report, and the coroner's, with the dental records. They wouldn't need their own team to check what the…"

I had stopped listening. Dental records? Involuntarily, my tongue had shot to the empty space at the back of my upper teeth, and then across to the matching space on the other side. Something seemed to crawl up my back.

Scott had warned me that those wisdom teeth needed to come out without delay.

And, nearly three months ago, he'd pulled them.

For half price.

Because I was a friend.

24.

The breeze had freshened and some of the treetops were beginning to sway.

"Dental records–how did that work?"

"I was here when Scott came to tell me he was going to have to do that. I don't know–only what Scott told me."

"Which was?"

Which, when I pressed her, was just about everything: Scott must have bragged about it. He could make new dental notations for himself to match my jaw and the actual teeth the police would be examining. But, like all his patients, Scott and I each had large gray cards that held little bite-wing X-rays of our teeth, side by side and in order. Faking that was a little harder. Scott and I both had pretty regular teeth, so Scott would use my X-rays as his own just by destroying or hiding his and slipping my films into the little slots for them on the back of the card with his name. But years earlier he'd had four wisdom teeth pulled, and my body would still have those teeth. Yes, he could substitute my X-rays for his in those slots, just like all the others, but that was chancy because all his staff would know he was missing those teeth–he sometimes pointed it out to patients if he was urging them to have wisdom teeth pulled. And, Linda, his dental hygienist, worked on Scott's teeth as well as on his patients'. She'd know for sure. When the staff looked up his files to give to the cops, someone could notice. There was no easy way for Scott to fake that–so my teeth had to come out.

"Laura, that's the lowest thing I've ever come across in my life. And for a day after it hurt like hell!"

She tried pleading. "But you have to know how cornered Scott felt by then. He came to Paris last month to tell me the insurance was our only way out. Things had gotten so bad he was making a deal to sell the beach house."

"Oh yeah? Let me tell you something. Scott had done that already–before we ever met him. I found three years of rent receipts in his desk. Apparently, he bought the house earlier, but then he sold it in 1965 and rented it back, around the time he moved to San Francisco."

Laura twisted in the seat and leaned forward accusingly, with a clenched fist on each knee. "You went through his private papers?"

"For Christ sakes–by then I'd put a girl in the bay! I found a can of gas where no one would just leave it. I thought Scott was in danger–they'd already botched killing him once. Sure I looked! I was so dumb I called my friend, Scott, to warn him. Then I had hours to wait around for him to get there. I'm a newsman–you think I wasn't curious? The real point is that Scott could have been in money trouble way before we met him. And here's something else. It was only about three weeks after I led a memorial service for *you* that he convinced me to pull those wisdom teeth. So he'd already done that that at least two months ago, long before he told you he was going to have to do it."

"But why lie to *me*?"

"Honey, Scott was an addict–you had to know that! How long do you think that $700,000 would have lasted you in Europe? Scott would put on a sharp suit and take you to Monte Carlo and win ten thousand at baccarat, then start dropping twenty every time they shuffled the cards. Keeping it secret was part of his fun."

"He lied to me?"

"Every kind of addict ends up lying. He sure lied to me about my teeth."

"Oh, stop!"

Out of nowhere, something that had surprised me before, came back to me and I changed the subject. "Laura, in one of your photos you were wearing a fur coat. Did Scott give you that?"

"For my birthday! It's mink!" She looked puzzled, but her answer was haughty enough.

"Do you have it now?"

"No. Scott does! Did. We kept it in his closet; I could hardly bring it home for you to see!"

"I guess not. But it was worth a lot. He could have brought it to you in his luggage when he came to Paris last month. I don't think he could just ship something overseas that might lead the cops to either of you."

"Who cares? Summer's coming. Maybe it's in cold storage."

"Or, and I'm just guessing here, maybe it's back in a shop that rents fancy stuff for special occasions. He leased his house, he leased his car. A mink, why not? His whole life was just a stage set. He could put on a new play every month. And, hey, look! I can't say he was lying to you about the guy in the parking lot who threatened him with your photo, but he could have been–he could have just bought the photo himself. No way to know now"

"I don't–"

"But he sure wanted to scare you enough to get you out of his way while he did what he wanted to me. He might've had me fooled, but he was fooling you too!

Laura leaned forward in the passenger seat for a moment with her head down, considering. Then she straightened up and opened the glove box. I thought she needed a tissue, but her hand came back out with a pistol in it. She gave me a matter-of-fact look that seemed to have no content at all.

"All right," she said, backing out of the car with the gun leveled at me. "You've left me nothing–no choice. Open the door and get out. Don't face me–just keep looking away but move to the right until you're away from the car." Her voice had no trace of emotion.

I tried to stall. "I saw a gun like that one the other day–but with a silencer."

"We bought a pair at a Reno gun show," she said. "For protection. Now do what I said. It's loaded."

Feeling empty inside, I did as I was told. So the attractive girl I'd met at the freshman mixer was going to kill me. All I could do was hope it was quick.

"Laura–" I said.

"Quiet! Don't turn around!" She was somewhere behind me, from the sound of it maybe fifteen feet away. Too far! I didn't trust her aim. I'd always feared hurting more than dying.

There was a sharp bang, a crack like a big branch breaking. She'd missed! You don't hear the shot that kills you! But I stood stock still waiting for the second–I might save myself now if I could dodge and run, but fear froze me in place. I waited, waited… "Look, Laura–"

No answer. I had to take a chance. I leaped to the left and spun around.

Laura had vanished!

No.

But she was gone all the same.

In her green dress, she had fallen into the long grass, partly obscured, so for just a moment I hadn't been able to register that my 'late wife' was now dead.

25.

I needn't have worried about her aim. One look told me that she'd put the muzzle in her mouth. I didn't look a second time—or touch her. I left the gun where it had fallen. Sitting under a tree 40 feet away, with my head on my knees, I grieved for her a second time. What had she said? "It all went so wrong!" But not just their nasty plot—our marriage too.

Her suicide was the last thing I had wanted, the last thing I'd expected when I followed her to Paris. I couldn't bring myself to hate my own wife even after she'd betrayed me, but I did see that everything that had happened to her had been her own doing. I had felt guilty about her death months ago, when it didn't happen, but now I felt only relief that I was alive.

Ten minutes must have gone by before I looked up, and then at my watch. It was mid-afternoon already. I wasn't going wait for someone to find us together, and I wasn't going to lead the gendarmes to Laura and again risk becoming the only suspect. She was a suicide with fake ID. Someone else could report the body. I went to the Mercedes and opened the back door using my handkerchief, still pointlessly worrying about fingerprints. This rental car might have the prints of 30 drivers. I grabbed my little briefcase-bag, and started off through the trees, but I didn't get thirty feet before I whirled and went back to the car. I had to look at Laura's fake ID. What if Scott had listed her as Mrs. Gregory Johnson? Now that was my identity too, and anyone might follow that paper trail through airports and to me.

So–the handkerchief again–I opened the passenger door. Laura's dark green leather purse still sat on the floor in front of her seat, next to the gear shift hump. I pawed through it until I had her billfold and driver's license–from Louisiana this time–with her photo, a good one I'd never seen. Relief! Her fake name was Eloise Pierce, surely one she wouldn't have chosen for herself. So perhaps her identity had belonged to someone already dead.

I did my best to wipe or smear fingerprints on the billfold and bag, close the car door and set off on foot again in the direction we'd been driving. I didn't intend to be spotted on the same road, and the woods couldn't last forever.

They lasted longer than I expected, though, and at one point I had to jump a wide creek–crooked, but slow and muddy like an irrigation ditch. For most of the way the woods were civilized–almost a park, but with uneven ground and long grass. And that spring they were full of life. Just hiking through I flushed out more quail, chased two squirrels up trees, nearly stepped on a frog at the creek and convinced myself that I heard larger creatures moving ominously somewhere–but probably that part was only nerves. Just then I also understood that the woods were full of death.

26.

To think about death was to think about survival. After Laura's 'fatal car crash,' it was Scott himself who had told me that I was a survivor, and that survivors had to think ahead and not back. I had no plan for the spot I was in, so I needed to think ahead now.

After what seemed about two miles I was beginning to wonder if I was walking in circles even though there was no chance of that because the sun was still ahead of me, so I was heading west. Eventually the trees began to thin and I could see a meadow or pasture in the distance with a low stone wall on the far side, and beyond that an occasional car passing.

Crossing that field I was still working out the story I'd need to get a ride after I vaulted the wall and got to the road. My high school French wouldn't help much.

Once I was beside the narrow highway, carrying my fabric briefcase, I started north because I'd driven south. I'd only gotten about a hundred yards when an old blue Citroen passed me, slowed and stopped just ahead. I caught up, went to the open passenger window and saw a smiling, bald young man, apparently East Indian, with a head the shape, color and sheen of a brown olive. He wore a dark business suit, white shirt and a solid-purple tie.

"*Bonjour, Monsieur!*" I said, "*Je voudrait un*–uh–ride…"

"Ah, you speak English! Get in." he replied. "I can take you as far as Orly–the town, not the airfield. What are you doing alone and walking on the verge?" His English sounded very British to me.

"I had an old friend who died in the town south of here today," I said. "I just flew in this morning, but I was too late–he was already gone. His brother drove me to the last turn-off. I'm really kind of lost now. I can't even remember the name of that town."

"Corbiel?'

"That's it, Corbiel! Thanks."

"I'm sorry for your loss–and to have flown all the way from–?"

"New York."

"Ah, all night then; you must be tired."

"Now that you say it, I think I am–very. I could use a hotel room and a nap, but, really, I need to arrange a flight back to the U.S. I had expected to be here longer."

He shot me a quizzical sidelong glance. "But you have only this small bag?"

Uneasy as that made me, I could answer with the truth. "I was in a hurry. 'Left my suitcase at the airport. I plan to get it later."

"Ah!" he said flashing a broad smile. "My name is P. K. Pushpa. Perhaps I can be of some help. I happen to be the head of reception at the Hotel Agenta in Orly. My work begins in half an hour and I'm on my way there. We are not a large establishment, but usually quite acceptable to tourists. I can take you there now, if you like, Mr. –"

"Greg Johnson," I said. "That would be wonderful! Thank you. I'll pay for the night, but I may leave early if I can get a flight."

"Perhaps I can even assist you with that. I am not only the Agenta's evening reception agent, but also its concierge!" he said with obvious pride. "We see many guests going directly to the airfield, so we have the official book of flight schedules. I've often helped people arrange travel. There will be a number of airline choices to New York."

"You are a marvel!" I said. "Thank you!" But my easy lie about flying from New York necessitated another: "However, I really need a flight to San Francisco now, because I was due there today for an educators' conference. I canceled that to fly to Paris, but I should get to the rest of the conference if I can."

"Probably no non-stops, but we can look."

"Thanks!"

Pushpa was a stroke of luck for me, I thought, but at the same time I was at his mercy, and again I felt like a fugitive. If Laura's body was found soon and the news spread, he might think about where I had joined him and reconsider my story. And if he called the authorities his hotel would be holding me as surely as if I were in lockup. It wouldn't do to be nervous. I had to brazen it out and hope for the best. Looking for a safe gambit, I said, "May I compliment you on your English? You are easier to understand than some of my friends in America."

"Thank you very much, indeed," he said. You know, English is sure to be India's first language soon. The students in my school spoke nothing else. My father jokes with his Paris colleagues that India is saving English *from* the English.

"Your family is in Paris?"

"My father is in the employ of the Indian Embassy." he said. "Do you know what he does?"

"What?"

"He's a spy!"

Shocked at his openness, I turned to look at him, but he was already smiling at his own joke. "In the Cold War, everyone in every Embassy in Paris is a spy–at least that's what everyone in every other embassy believes!"

I chuckled. Appreciatively.

27.

We were approaching Orly, an old town of perhaps twenty to thirty thousand people, at a guess. Pushpa said it had seen a lot of Nazi uniforms during World War II, because the airfield had been taken over by the Luftwaffe. "That's history here now," he said. "I was still a little kid in Delhi at the end of the war."

"The airport seemed really busy this morning."

"Too busy probably. But Paris is building a bigger one north of town now."

We rode quietly after that. I didn't want to attempt small talk at the moment, and perhaps Pushpa was respecting my half-lie about the death of my "friend."

The Hotel Agenta, when we reached it down a cobbled street, turned out to be a narrow brick building, just four windows wide above street level, and five stories tall. An elderly woman at a small old-fashioned switchboard greeted us. Pushpa introduced her as Madame Neyon, consulted the register, hesitated for a moment over my bearded passport photo, then accepted it without a word. He registered me by my alias and showed me to an elevator scarcely large enough for a family of four–fewer with luggage. On the fourth floor he led me to a room, clean and with a window on the street, but with no space to spare. It held a double bed against the wall with the window, a small table, a chair and a tall chest in place of a closet. No place even to consider putting a television set. It was fortunate that Scott's suitcase was still at the airport because I'd have had to keep it on the bed or step over it to get to the bath.

Thankfully, the windowless bath was the same size as the bedroom and had a large claw-foot tub.

"I think I'll have a bath first thing," I said. "And then I'll need to find somewhere to eat–my last meal was breakfast on the plane."

Pushpa looked at a pocket watch on a black cord. "Four-fifteen–much too early for dinner anywhere, but the bars will be open, and it's tea-time for the British–there's an English tea shop one street to the east."

So, having washed away the grime of travel, polished the dust off my shoes, and wearing the only fresh shirt in my carry-on, I had British High Tea–finger sandwiches with cucumber slices, fish paste or cheese; scones with clotted cream and excellent jam; petits fours and a strong and fragrant pot of Earl Grey, my only meal in the heart of France.

I was feeling the weight of the day, and probably jet lag, and was ready for sleep when I returned to the hotel but was glad when Pushpa stopped me at the front desk. "I've been looking for San Francisco flights," he said. 'Nothing nonstop, I'm afraid, and most flights don't leave here until mid-morning, so you lose a day at your conference. But if you're willing to switch airlines in London there's an Air France flight to London Heathrow at about 11:30 tonight. There's a two-hour layover there, but you could fly out of London on Trans World with a short stop in New York and be at your San Francisco conference before noon."

"Teriffic! Thanks for the trouble."

"And you'd would be wise to take that one. Air service may become a problem any day now–ground crews are beginning to talk about striking. Shall I call to reserve tickets? What class would you want?"

"Tourist–that'll be pricy enough at the last minute. But

warn them I have no traveler's checks, only cash. I was in a hurry."

"You can exchange dollars for francs at the airport if you're early enough. It's just after 6. I'll call for a taxi at 9:30 latest and send Jacque, the bellman, up to wake you before that."

I slouched in a lobby chair until Pushpa had confirmed the reservation, then went up to my room, found a Hotel Agenta envelope in the drawer of my little table, wrote "Thanks!" across a sheet of Agenta stationery, folded $100 of Scott's cash into it and slipped the sealed envelope into my coat pocket along with a loose ten dollar bill to offer for 'gas money.' Pushpa had gone out of his way for me, and I hated to deceive him. There was no real reason to get to San Francisco before noon tomorrow, but there was every reason to get out of France as soon as I could.

I shrugged out of my coat, pulled my shoes and trousers off and fell into the bed exhausted.

28.

When a soft rap on the door didn't wake me, someone in the hall had unlocked my door, entered my room and was shaking my shoulder. I popped awake. Had the police come for me? Who was attacking? But it was only Pushpa.

"Time to dress," he said. "I think it will be necessary for me to drive you to the airport myself. I called for a taxi, but there is not one to be had in Orly at this hour. The dispatcher says all the drivers are meeting right now to consider joining the strikers."

"Oh, but I hate to put you out after all you've done."

"What I've done will be worthless if you can't make your plane. Jacque can handle the desk. There is really no other way–by the way, it's raining."

Okay, I'll get ready."

"Good, meet me at the front door. I'll bring the car around."

In the rain, streetlights were making the cobblestones shine like polished onyx when I lifted my carry-on back into the old Citroen.

"You should be early enough to reclaim your luggage and exchange dollars for francs," Pushpa said, shifting into gear, "but things are in such turmoil today it will be well to have a margin of time."

"So the workers are beginning to join the students?"

"Some are. There is some serious hard feeling toward the state today. Last night there was a riot in the Latin Quarter and hundreds–hundreds–are in hospitals today.

The students claim the gendarmes took over a peaceful rally, that they used agent provocateurs posing as students."

"What's it all about, Pushpa, just trying to bring down de Gaulle?"

"Everyone in France has a different answer. Mine is that it's not so much political as social. The students are tired of just listening to lectures. They want to be able to ask questions, and that's not how teaching here has been done. I see it as young against old. The young are impatient. They insist on change and want their share. The old are settled and determined to keep what they have. They resist even change that is inevitable. When the riots have cost everyone more than they can afford, both sides will withdraw and go back to grumbling. It's too bad you had to see France this way–it's a wonderful country."

"Well, I'll be back someday."

Pushpa's explanation didn't sound convincing to me, though it was no doubt right as far as it went. But, after all, he'd just told me that everyone in France had a different answer.

The rain was softening and Pushpa switched the wipers to slow as he drove down the approach to the terminal. When we turned into the street beside the long building, it was a bright glare in the rain from the rows of fluorescent ceiling lights inside and yellow turn signals and red taillights in the street.

"Air France's ticket desk is about here," Pushpa said as he drove, "and then comes the foreign exchange, but I'm dropping you at baggage to reclaim your suitcase first."

I clutched the carry-on and hopped out as soon as the car stopped.

"Pushpa, thank you for everything! "Here's ten dollars for the gas and here's a message to open when you get back to the hotel."

He smiled, nodded and slipped the bill and envelope into his coat pocket.

"*Au revoir, mon ami!*" I said.

He flashed a grin. "Goodbye and good luck."

I ducked for shelter and the Citroen pulled out into the stream of taillights.

The baggage handlers pointed me toward the Left-Luggage Room and a dark-skinned attendant there took my luggage claim ticket, went down the row of shelves marked with the symbols of different airlines, and quickly returned with the suitcase. I didn't yet have francs, but he smiled broadly when I tipped him a dollar, so it was apparently enough.

At the foreign exchange kiosk, I was third in a line that moved quickly, and a gray little Frenchman, who smelled of an infusion of alcohol with his dinner, accepted some of Scott's hundred-dollar bills for the francs I would need for tickets on two carriers.

I cursed Scott's leather suitcase as I lugged it toward Air France ticket counters. I carried it with my right hand, but that meant shifting the briefcase bag to my left and that wrist was still sore enough to notice. There was not a thing in the suitcase that I wanted to keep, but it could be a mistake to leave it behind. Once in San Francisco, I thought, I would box up everything and drop it at a thrift store pick-up spot. Someone would inherit some pretty expensive clothes.

I had hoped to see Paris by night flying out, but what I saw in the rain was a hazy cover that seemed to be briefly illuminated in pastels from below. So I told myself that I had "seen Paris" flying in; I had just never really been there yet.

Air France's Vickers propjet took me to London Heathrow in just under two hours of flying time, but only one by the clock, because we had gained an hour crossing a time zone. The engines were smooth and quiet compared to the 707's, but it was an unsettling time for me. I shut my eyes and expected to sleep but, after napping for an hour or so at Pushpa's hotel, I ended up just brooding.

So far, I had been thinking of the rain in France only as an inconvenience, but now I began to see it in a way that made me the curator of my own personal museum of horrors. The woods where I had parked the Mercedes looked made for a picnic–they certainly weren't as wild as California forests. Still, for the hour and a half Laura and I had talked there in the car, not a soul had come along. So now I imagined that Laura's body was still lying in the cold rain, and even worse, I dreamed up unlikely predator animals waiting for the rain to stop. I had left her, I had left Misty, I had left Scott–I'd fled every time, and I felt that I deserved to be branded a coward for life. But I resented that, too. I hadn't asked for any of it and thinking about Scott made it easier to be more angry than ashamed. He'd caused it all. I owed him nothing. I was shaken by Laura's death, but she herself had chosen to do everything she had done, right to the end. And I told myself again that Misty was their victim, not mine.

As I reflected on what I knew now that I had not known when I left San Francisco Saturday morning, I also saw that, when I drove into the Chevron Station in Los Gatos there had been no hitchhiker with a thumb out waiting for just any ride that came along. But when I left the restroom minutes later and returned to my fancy car, there was Misty, perfumed and posed beside my exit to the road. So I could forget the idea that I had unwittingly lured her to her death.

Knowing this didn't make me feel any wiser, but it stiffened my spine to be a little less gullible in the future.

29.

London Heathrow after midnight was more cavernous than Orly, busy but also quieter, less crowded. I had a nearly two-hour wait, so on my way through the terminal I stopped at a Smith's news shop and bought *The Times*, *The Guardian* and the tabloid *Sun*. When I came to a nearly empty pub, I went in and picked out a simple pub grub meal and–the best of it–a bottle of Worthington's Pale Ale. It occurred to me as I sat finishing the ale that I had been to France without having a glass of wine. Then I leafed through all three papers, but, as I'd expected, any follow-up story about the murder of a San Francisco "socialite dentist" was nowhere to be found. There was plenty on the Paris riots, however–*The Manchester Guardian* said as many as 400 had been hospitalized on Monday alone.

My plane was already outside and under floodlights when I reached TWA's boarding area, another Boeing 707, this one glossy white from nose to tail. The waiting area was filling up, and the crowd, by this forth leg of my trip, seemed familiar–a different airline and route, but the same business suits that I had seen coming to Europe, the same combination of bored waiting-room faces and travelers anticipating adventure.

It was good to know that flying west I'd get home in fewer hours on the clock than the flight would really take; I wanted those hours back. I had never in my life thought I would be glad to leave Paris behind, but It was a relief now just to be in Britain, and New York would be better yet.

When we boarded, despite the hour, tourist class was

almost full. My seat was even closer to the back, 26C, on the aisle, and the smell of cigarette smoke was heavy there, but I was used to it; I worked in a newspaper city room after all. There were already occupants in 26A and 26B: a tall young Middle Eastern-looking man at the window and a sturdy woman in the center seat, probably in her late fifties. She had curly steel-colored hair that reminded me of a scouring pad, and the fine lines that converged at the corners of her eyes suggested lots of close reading.

I introduced myself as Greg Johnson and she told me she was Martha Prince, flying home to San Francisco after a month-long vacation in Italy, France and England.

"I'm surprised the plane is so nearly full at this hour," I said.

"Well, it is cheaper than the morning flights and that can matter to tourists. And, if you can sleep on the plane you save a night's hotel bill. It gets into New York at a good time, too–the start of the day. I used a Eurail Pass and had a wonderful time here, but I'll be happy to have lunch with friends in San Francisco today.

"What do you do in San Francisco?" I asked.

"For years I taught history at Lick High until they tore it down for the expressway. Now I teach at Balboa. European history is my specialty, so this trip is one I always wanted to make."

"But you're here early–isn't school still under way?"

"Not for me. I took the year off to care for my husband, Paul, who was ill. Unfortunately, I lost him early in the school year."

"Oh! I'm very sorry."

"Me too." She said it a second time, more thoughtfully, "Me too." Then she brightened, "But now I've done what he told me to do. I've used a bit of the insurance money he left to see the lands I've been teaching about all these years. I had hoped to go to Europe right out of college, but it didn't work out."

"You couldn't go later?"

"A teacher's salary doesn't make it easy."

"So now that you've been to Europe, would you teach any differently?"

She liked that question–her eyes lit up and she nodded enthusiastically. "Yes, quite a bit, I think."

"How so?"

"Well, I'll spend less time on kings and battles, and more on how people lived–on artists and miners and inventors. I'm already making lesson plans. I'd teach more about daily lives, how hard it was to build cathedrals and how dedicated and patient the people were who did it, and about robbers on the road, and traveling bands of players in morality plays–all of that."

"That class sounds fascinating."

"Well, I hope to make it inspiring. I don't see many kids who'll grow up to be kings, but there are a lot who have it in them to be actors or inventors or engineers."

After that, Martha Prince and I chatted through takeoff and until the plane leveled off and the overhead cabin lights were dimmed. Then she turned on the little spotlight over her tray table, put her book on it and read. I leaned back and tried to think only ahead. But it was not long until I dozed off.

* * *

I was fighting for my life in the dark! Scott had one hand on my throat, and I was flat on my back, swinging the iron wildly, when my hand flew open and the iron vanished out of it. "Now!" he said and I felt the cold muzzle of the big pistol against my cheek. I knew I was on my last breath when–suddenly–the floor came apart under us and we both tumbled down, down through blackness until my eyes flew open as we thumped heavily against something soft.

In the dimly lit cabin of the 707, people around me were gasping and starting to talk urgently to each other. There was the familiar ping or chime, the "Fasten Seat Belt" light came on and then, on the sound system, the captain's calm voice: "Sorry for that sudden drop, folks. We encountered a little unanticipated turbulence. We do expect to have quieter air ahead, but please fasten your seat belt as a precaution and stay seated until the sign goes off. Flight attendants, please do a cabin check."

The young women in their crisp twill uniforms were already moving up the aisle, looking right and left at every row and reassuring nervous passengers. Up front a baby had begun to cry.

Over the engine noise, I heard a woman behind me say, "I thought we were going down!" A concerned male voice answered her: "Honey, everyone was scared–it was sudden. But we're okay, we're okay!"

Martha Prince turned to me: "You must have a sixth sense. Just before that jolt you gave a big gasp in your sleep and seemed to know it was coming."

"Huh...maybe. I think I was just having a nightmare. But I fell in that too, and woke up when we hit, so who knows?"

"I read somewhere that in a dream you fall but never hit anything–just falling wakes you."

"I didn't know that. But maybe I woke before the thump. I definitely felt it, like everybody else."

"I thought it was scary," Martha said, "But the pilot seemed almost bored–terribly formal."

"I think they must learn that at flight school to calm passengers, maybe even have a script of some kind. It's a good bet we're never going to hear a pilot come on and say, 'Holy mackerel, folks! That was a close call!'"

Martha chuckled, but with her lips pressed together tight, as if she didn't want to acknowledge a dumb joke from an unruly student.

"To be honest, for a moment I thought we could die," she said.

"Well, we're fine now."

She gave me a rueful smile and a grimace, nodded, then went back to her book, under its little spotlight.

We could have died, I thought.

30.

I could have died. After all I'd survived, that would have been a pretty grim joke on me.

Still, being gone was somehow seductive to contemplate. What if I never showed up at work again? How would that play out? What if I *had* died somehow, just not in a jet crash. No one but Pushpa knew I was on this flight, and he didn't know my real name, so what if I'd just disappeared?

Well, at the *Record* they'd call my apartment and get no answer. Eventually someone would open the place up and find it untouched since Saturday morning, my framed photo of Laura still on the dresser. What then?

Suddenly I stumbled on pieces of Scott's mendacity I'd overlooked. He'd told me to keep mum about using his house because he didn't want friends to know he was lending it to me so freely. Falling for that also meant that no one would know later I had even been there. He'd done his best to see that I didn't shop at a local grocery, or wander around Monterey meeting other people, either. Once again, I had been such a patsy!

So there would be no obvious starting place to hunt for me. No one at the *Record* knew I had driven to Monterey and no one had any idea I'd been to Paris. But eventually my Ford would show up, still parked at the airport. Oh–with the note in the glove box still–the one Scott typed above my signature, suggesting but not spelling out that I was too weak to go on without Laura. The conceit of that was galling–as if either of them was worth more than life to me–not now they weren't!

The kid's bike would still be in the back of the car too. No telling what someone would make of that.

But the note might mean one thing if the car was next to the Golden Gate Bridge when I went missing, and another now when it was in an airport long-term parking lot–maybe I'd flown out of SFO, but maybe I'd just walked over to the taxi rank and grabbed a cab to the bridge–or anywhere else. Anywhere! Cold trail. No clue at the ticket counters. No ticket in my name.

So where could I go? Anywhere as Gregory Johnson, with a passport, driver's license and social security card to match. And if I grew a beard and styled it the same way I'd look even more like an older version of the young guy in the photo.

But I'd have to pick a new airline. 'Just get off this plane, look at the departures board and see what's leaving soon. Delta to Atlanta–too far today after the long flight from Paris. United or Continental to Denver. American to Phoenix. Pacific Southwest to Los Angeles?

PSA? Maybe.

I didn't really want another flight today, but it would be over in an hour and a half. Soon after that I could be having a room service dinner in one of the big hotels near the L.A. airport. Tomorrow I could rest there all day and on Friday I could fly out again, anywhere in the country. I've never been to Miami, for example. But, of course, eventually I'll need to end up near Hartford, with the beard I'll grow by then, because that'll be the whole point–to show up as Greg Johnson, the unexpected beneficiary of poor Scott Croswell, killed by a thug or thugs in California. I'll have to wait a decent time and think everything through, but I can collect my inheritance from two $350,00 policies.

Let's see, with Guild scale and a merit raise and overtime the *Record-Courier* is now paying me almost $17,000 a year, and I'm living well enough. But things keep getting more expensive. As a kid in the late '40s, I was sent to the store with twenty cents for a loaf of bread. And now some loaves cost as much as a dollar. So, 700,000 loaves? That's a lot of bread.

It's no secret that my life has been a bit dismal since Laura vanished out of it. I like my work, but the hours aren't great if you'd like to get out in the evening. With $700,000 in the bank I don't think I'd have much trouble keeping more evenings work-free.

And speaking of bread–bread attracts birds, as the British say. Some bright, nice-looking lady a lot less avaricious than Misty might still be more interested in me if I'm not living almost paycheck to paycheck. I have an automatic deduction for savings at the *Record's* credit union, but what's there–$3,200 maybe? How many times could you divide $700,000 by that?

Or, Suppose Greg Johnson eventually flew back to Paris after things there were back to normal, and got a tryout on the copy desk of the Paris *Herald Tribune*? Even when you just saw it from the air, Paris was beautiful. Why couldn't I have a dream job–and a dream apartment–in Paris for a few years?

On the other hand, with a lot less than $700,000 I could even *buy* a weekly newspaper, in some little New England town, for example, or anywhere else. I could set my own hours, long hours, of course, but I was born to be an editor. I'll be a big fish in a small pond, make a name for myself–well, for Greg Johnson, anyway.

Scott had set up his get-rich scheme with me as the fall guy; it was all going to be at my expense. But when I messed it up, it turned out that I was the one who could end up rich. That didn't seem like larceny to me, it seemed like justice. Just yesterday, I had used Scott's money to rent a hotel room, buy a meal, tip Pushpa, and get plane tickets, and none of that bothered my conscience a bit. As for the insurance company—well, all the premiums have been kept up on both policies. They have to pay off if Scott dies, and Scott's dead—big headlines tell you that. The payoff is just money owed to the named beneficiary, Greg Johnson. And that's me; I have the I.D. to prove it.

The truth is, Scott and Laura both deserved it for what they had tried to do to me. So once again it's karma! San Francisco to L.A. today, Miami no later than Friday night, stay as long as you like, wing it after that. Buy a car, maybe, and drive all the way up the Atlantic coast? The biggest unknown will be waiting to see how long it takes my beard to grow.

31.

The thump of the wheels on the runway roused me when we landed in New York. Planning my new life, I had eventually drowsed off, and now I'd missed seeing the city from the air. The Middle Eastern man in the seat next to Martha had raised the shade and I could see just that it was early light but overcast. On the intercom, the flight attendant welcomed us to New York, said that local time was 5:50 a.m. and urged "those going on to San Francisco" to stay on board, we would be here only 40 minutes.

I was curious about the airport, I'd been here once when it was named Idlewild, but a few years after that it became Kennedy and I knew there were some brand-new terminals. Still, ever since I had left San Francisco on Monday, my nights' sleeps had been no more than naps. It was early morning and I was bushed. I drowsed again, dimly aware of passengers filing off and new ones filing on, until we pushed back for takeoff. Once we were in the air, from my aisle seat I got just a glimpse of the overcast New York skyline, standing up in silhouette as in a black-and-white movie. Then I settled back for a six-or-seven-hour flight to San Francisco.

* * *

Early in 1964, just nine days after I started at the *Record* as a general assignment reporter, Ed Harris, the city editor, sent me to interview Dennis Crowley, a San Francisco councilman who'd come close to dying two weeks before.

Crowley, a big man, had gone striding across the floor under the City Hall rotunda and up the ornate marble

157

staircase that leads to the second floor when he felt a burning pain in his chest and had to sit down quick. The aide who was with him raced up the steps and into the mayor's outer office, grabbed the receptionist's phone and called for paramedics. They were there in six minutes, put nitroglycerine under his tongue and took him to the Emergency Room at Saint Luke's, where it turned out he hadn't yet had a heart attack but was on the edge of one. His angiogram test the next day showed that stents wouldn't be enough–he needed a double bypass, which turned out to be a triple when the surgeons finally opened up his chest. But eight days after that, Crowley was recuperating in his condo on the side of Mt. Davidson, out of danger, itching to get back to work.

Crowley was a well-known advocate for the South-of-Market-Street redevelopment project that was being hotly debated all over the city just then, and Ed got the idea to have me to do a feature on what matters most to someone who's had a brush with death. "Be sure to ask him if the South-of-Market debate matters less to him now," Ed told me.

I called to set up an interview, and the next day Crowley, lumbering a little, opened the door for me himself. We sat at his kitchen table while he finished a bowl of chicken soup for lunch. I told him he looked pretty good for a man with staples in his chest.

He grinned. "Funny about that," he said. "I already feel almost good enough to drive, but I really can't for nearly a month. My ribs have to grow back together. If I drove now and got into even a little rear-ender, the steering wheel could knock the ribs right into my lungs, puncture 'em and–just like that–I'd be a gonner! I was planning to sneak out and tool around town until they laid that on me."

Halfway through the interview, I asked Ed's question:

"What about the big battle over the South-of-Market project? Does that seem less important to you than it did before?"

"Oh hell no!" Crowley said. "That was important before I thought I was dying, and it's just as important as ever now that I'm not. What's changed for me are just little things I didn't really appreciate before. They mean a lot more now."

"Such as?"

"Well, on sunny mornings I like to sit out on my balcony here, just looking out over the city and having my coffee. 'Done it for years. Sometimes my big yellow cat, Oleo, comes out and sits on the deck right beside my chair, and sometimes I reach down and scratch her behind the ears. That's always been nice enough, but as I was doing that this morning, I realized it was nothing but pure pleasure now. I can't tell you how wonderful it is to feel the warm sun, sip coffee, and hear a big cat purr while you rub its head. That's a whole different thing after you believed you wouldn't even be here this week."

That was my lead, of course:

> Councilman Dennis Crowley knows now what matters most after a near-death experience and it's not life's big projects, but something as simple as the pure pleasure that comes from sitting in the sun, sipping coffee and petting a big purring cat.
>
> "That's a whole different thing after you believed you wouldn't even be here this week," he says.

I can still recall that lead word-for-word because it got me my first Page One byline at the *Record-Courier*.

I was remembering it now because the scent of coffee brewing in the galley was beginning to fill the cabin of the 707, and I was enjoying how remarkably fresh it smelled–better than coffee had ever smelled before–and how good it felt not to be dead and to know that I had no real intention of murdering myself.

I was damned if I'd be Greg Johnson for the rest of my life!

* * *

From the first, I've tried here to tell only what I believed when I believed it, what I learned when I learned it and what I felt as I felt it. So, my plan to take over Scott's plot and collect a big insurance prize for myself was as real as everything else to me. It happened just as I said–but only in my head–a plan I got deep into during a long night as I sat in seat 26C of an airliner flying west ahead of the sun. You don't see the sun rise when you fly west overnight, but eventually daylight creeps up on you, and then imagining yourself living inside a lie gets harder to do.

Yes, I thought about the big money I could be leaving on the table, but the truth is it didn't matter that much to me. If you decided to be a newsman, you weren't like guys in college who set out to be engineering hot shots or Madison Avenue ad men. Just going in you had to know you weren't very likely to get rich. For this job, truth had to matter to you more than dollars. So lying about your own name–your byline–wouldn't cut it.

* * *

When it came, breakfast was terrific: hot coffee, fresh orange juice, strawberry yogurt, Canadian bacon, scrambled eggs and warm flaky biscuits with butter and two tiny grey pots of Dundee marmalade and French cherry jam. I ate it all. It tasted so good I wondered what more they could be getting in First Class, and, whatever it was, I didn't even envy them.

By the time the breakfast trays were gone, the snowy peaks of the Rockies were below us, reflecting the brilliant morning sun. It was a beautiful day! I had reset my watch to local time in New York, and now it read 10:10, so I set it back three hours for San Francisco, 7:10 a.m. Beside me, Martha Prince had put her book down, opened a stenographer's notebook and was scribbling intently.

"Lesson plans?" I asked her.

"Well, notes for them, anyway. I don't want to lose these ideas when I have them."

"I'll leave you alone, then."

"Thanks! I can't tell you how much I'm looking forward to being in the classroom with my kids."

Martha was a strong woman, I thought. And we had something in common–she'd lost her husband early in the school year; I'd lost my wife in January...and for good just yesterday. But we'd both be going back to jobs we loved.

When I thought about it, as different as they were, all the women I'd come across recently showed signs of being pretty independent one way or another. Bob Dylan's song was right: "The Times, They Are a Changing."

Take that stewardess–Annie. Twenty years back she would have come out of school and found a husband to 'provide' for her. Now she was happily doing a demanding, even potentially dangerous, job with lots of self-confidence. She could clearly take care of herself. You had to admire that.

When we were above the Sierra Nevada, the speakers came on and the captain told us he expected on-time arrival at 10:05. I had gotten into London just after midnight on Thursday morning and–eight time zones later–it was still Thursday morning.

I knew I had jet lag, but now it felt like something more, and as if it dated all the way back to Saturday, when I had first settled into the Porsche. My weariness had put me into a kind of trance, but at the same time, I had been through so much that just flying out of it all made me ecstatic.

I was due back at work at 3 p.m. Saturday. So I had three days to sleep, to sort it all out, and to vow never to tell, to those I knew, what I knew. I probably would have more nightmares ahead; I had been through a real one, after all. They might dog me for a while. I'd just have to wait them out.

"There's the Bay!" Martha said suddenly. I half-stood in my seat to look over her to see water sparkling to the south of us.

"That very last row of seats behind us is empty," I said. "I'm going back there to look." The whine of the engines dropped and, just as I took the window seat, the plane banked to the left and the wing dipped so that I was looking into the water as we turned south.

For the next quarter-hour we flew lower and lower over the familiar cities on the east side of the Bay, past Vallejo, Berkeley, Oakland, with its big ship-loading docks across the estuary from Alameda, then out over the milky green water of the South Bay and the long, low dogleg of the San Mateo Bridge, until we made a sweeping turn back to the north for final approach. After that I was facing the hills of the Peninsula, and, though we were too low now to see Skyline Boulevard, I was coming back home flying more or less parallel with it. As we dropped closer to landing, the plane began to slide and yaw a bit, just as the seagulls had above Skyline on Saturday. *We're riding the same wind*, I thought.

The 707 was settling into its low, over-water approach. Everything on the shore outside began to move faster; San

Mateo went by off to the left, then Burlingame, the cars in the airport's long-term lot, now the terminal beside us, the big plane shuddering as wheels touched tarmac, a smooth landing.

I was home and ready for a new start–not as the Man with the Porsche, not as Dan, as I'd told Misty, not as Gregory Johnson, the name on my passport, but as myself–as someone who understood how valuable it is just to be who you really are, with your own life to live.

I was glad I'd gassed up the Ford. I'd sleep today but when I woke tomorrow, I might get the classified ads and drive around looking for a different apartment, a place to make new memories. Who knew what I could do in time? Maybe I really could become a top editor soon, maybe I'd get a dog, find a girlfriend, marry, have kids, buy an old house and remodel it into a showplace, become an amateur astronomer. Maybe someday, years from now, our kids would throw a big party when Annie and I celebrated our 40th wedding anniversary. Why not? Maybe when I'd retired, when the cops hunting today for Scott Croswell's "mob killers" were no longer on the force, I'd put the whole story into a book just so it wouldn't go untold–I'd done the legwork, so I'd make the report.

I was so euphoric just then that I'd gotten way ahead of myself, I suppose. But, really, things could happen just that way, couldn't they?

Well, I was right about that.

ABOUT THE AUTHOR

This is a photo of, Stan Burroway, but you might not recognize him from it now. It was taken for a resumé in the 1960s, when he was about the same age as the narrator of this book. In the years since, he has had a long career in journalism, spending the final twenty as an assistant national editor of the Los Angeles Times, primarily overseeing the Times' domestic bureaus with the exception of Washington D.C. He now lives with his dog, Trouble, in Reno, and writes for pleasure.

Made in the USA
Middletown, DE
30 October 2021